LOADED

How was it that I had come to this place?

How was it that an ineffectual, overeducated, liberally minded ne'er-do-well like myself had come to such a pass—holding a loaded shotgun, kneeling in these Alabama woods on a hot summer night with thoughts of assault and murder in mind?

The man stirred, turned his back to me, and stared out into the dark. He began fishing in his pockets. He was going to light another cigarette. He fumbled and dropped the pack on the ground. Cursing, he bent over to pick them up.

Now was my chance.

SOUTHERN LATITUDES

STEPHEN J. CLARK

BERKLEY PRIME CRIME, NEW YORK

SOUTHERN LATITUDES

A Berkley Prime Crime Book / published by arrangement with the author

PRINTING HISTORY
Berkley Prime Crime mass-market edition / September 2002

Cover art by Kamil Vojnar.
Cover design by George Long.
Text design by Julie Rogers.

For information address: The Berkley Publishing Group, a division of Penguin Putnam Inc.,
375 Hudson Street, New York, New York 10014.

Visit our website at
www.penguinputnam.com

ISBN: 0-425-18637-7

Berkley Prime Crime Books are published by The Berkley Publishing Group, a division of Penguin Putnam Inc.,
375 Hudson Street, New York, New York 10014.

PRINTED IN THE UNITED STATES OF AMERICA

10 9 8 7 6 5 4 3 2 1

To Franni, who found me
when I was lost

The Aurora Borealis
would be visible tonight
were we further north
and free of city lights.
Southern latitudes
are not conducive
to seeing far or deeply.
Winters tepid and damp
without the clarifying cold
of arctic night.

I would to a weatherstation
in Point Barrow, Alaska,
to a Quonset hut
on snowy tundra,
to concern myself only
with a few salient numbers—
wind speed, temperature,
barometric pressure—
watching the millibars plummet
at the approach of cold fronts
spinning down off the pole
like pinwheels.
Nights season-long,
deep and funereal,
punctuated only
by the recalcitrant glow,
filling the sky
outside my window.

—Jacques Rambeau,
Vineyards of Wrath

PROLOGUE

In the Woods, Saturday Evening

IT was in the last days of my youth, or perhaps the beginning of my middle age, that, unaccountably, I found myself back in my hometown of Litchfield, Alabama. Most of us walk through our days obliviously, our lives passing us by as if in a dream. Only after decades have slipped by do we sometimes awaken and notice what we have come to. So it was with me. After years of sleepwalking, decades of dribbling time away in halfhearted relationships and unwanted jobs, after a life of indecision and regret and lost chances, I came to myself in the unlikeliest of places, here in the woods on a humid night in June.

I knelt in the tall grass along the highway, my father's shotgun cradled in the crook of my arm. The night was alive with the murmuring of cicadas, the croak of bullfrogs, the screech and caw of things that crawled and flew. The air hung warm and thick about me, as intimate as a lover's breath. I felt the gravel under my knee, the brush of the grass against my arms, the blood pounding in my neck. Around my right calf, tucked into my sock and taped around my ankle with masking tape, I felt my hunting knife, its steel cool against my skin.

I breathed deep, my lungs working smooth as a bellows. I felt poised, watchful. As my eyes adjusted to the dark, the black wall of woods before me separated into individual trees—second-growth pines and scrub oaks. The stars shone brightly across the dome of the sky. I lowered my head and crept into the woods.

I walked slowly, picking my footing carefully among the brambles and fallen branches, listening. The shotgun felt awkward riding in the crook of my arm, but it had a pleasing cool heft to it.

The woods ran perhaps a quarter-mile across here, tumbling down the slope to the flood plains that ran along the river. The ground was shot through with gullies and abrupt drops. I crept down the hill slowly, picking my way quietly.

Halfway down, I stopped, kneeling again to listen.

The rattle and hum of the woods continued, but from farther off I could hear the discordant noise of human voices, muffled but distinctive, and the mechanical hum of air-conditioning compressors.

I crept along carefully. At the bottom of the hill the woods ran on another hundred yards then ended at the edge of a huge expanse of blacktop. As I came near the edge of the woods, the warehouses came into view—gray looming shadows. I paused, hunkered down beside the trunk of an oak, peering out into the darkness.

The warehouse lay perhaps fifty feet away. At its far end, bathed in the pool of a floodlight, a black car sat parked. A stocky man in a dark suit sat with his back to me, one haunch perched on one of the car's front fenders. He stared watchfully out into the dark toward the usual approaches one would take coming there.

I squatted by the oak and felt my heart pounding. My mouth was dry, my hands shook a little. The masking tape wrapped around my ankle pulled at the hairs on my leg and began to itch terribly as sweat trickled down my legs.

The man on the car flicked the cigarette out into the night and shifted about on the fender. He cast a glance over his shoulder, then stood and began pacing in front of the car.

I fingered the shotgun. The gunmetal felt cool, the wooden stock smooth and textured. The nubby bark of the oak met my cheek as I leaned against the trunk, the woody green smell of the tree suddenly strong. I became aware what a solid living thing a tree was.

How was it that I had come to this place?

How was it that an ineffectual, overeducated, liberally minded ne'er-do-well like myself had come to such a pass—holding a loaded shotgun, kneeling in these Alabama woods on a hot summer night with thoughts of assault and murder in mind?

The man stirred, turned his back to me, and stared

out into the dark. He began fishing in his pockets. He was going to light another cigarette. He fumbled and dropped the pack on the ground. Cursing, he bent over to pick them up.

Now was my chance.

1

Tuesday Night, Four Days Earlier

I DROVE down the highway, headlights shining out into the dark, tires hissing over the wet blacktop. My police scanner crackled and sputtered. The heat had moderated after the storm and I could almost imagine a faint coolness in the air. The old Ford creaked down the highway, as if it knew the way to my father's fish camp after years of repetition.

Some local voices came on the police scanner. I could never remember the police's arcane numerical lingo, but when real trouble appeared, the code often fell away and one might hear actual English being spoken.

"What you got, Mobile 3?" a crisp Southern voice asked.

"Got me a boy hanging here," another voice replied.

"Hanging?"

"And he ain't moving much."

"Repeat your location, Mobile 3."

"State 71, about a mile past Jewel's package store. North side of the road."

"We'll send backup. Do you need an ambulance?"

"Can't see that'd do much good."

I accelerated and looked ahead. If I remembered this stretch, there was a turnoff that would take me over to Highway 71. I kicked on the high beams. After a few miles I finally picked out a battered green sign marking Palmer Knox Road. Three miles down it would run into 71.

Palmer Knox was a local boy who had pitched a few years in the big leagues back in the fifties. After blowing out his elbow, he had come back to Litchfield and coached the high school baseball team for twenty-some years. For this brief success and long years of service, they named this two-lane blacktop after him. He lived on it, third house on the left, retired for the last ten years, pulling in ESPN on his satellite dish and lobbing sliders into a pitchback in his yard.

I pulled the old Ford into a hard left turn. It groaned and bucked but held the road. Now if only I could remember in which direction Jewel's package store lay.

The chatter on the police scanner ran on, becoming more regimented and less communicative. I came over a small rise and caught a possum fixed stone-footed in my headlights. His eyes reflected the white-blue of the lights back at me. I swerved to avoid him, but he roused himself at the last moment and lunged, placing himself squarely in my path again. My wheels bumped over him. I peered out the rearview mirror, but he was lost in the darkness behind.

At Highway 71 I gambled on a right turn. After several miles in the dark I finally made out the red-and-blue strobing of a couple of sheriff's patrol cars. I pulled in at a respectable distance, got out, and surveyed the scene.

Three patrol cars were gathered around a huge oak that sat about ten yards off the highway. Uniformed figures milled about in the glare of headlights. Far off another siren screamed. I walked toward the oak, trying to stand as clear in the open as I could so I would not present an unwanted surprise.

Someone came out at me from the dark. "Just where you think you're going?" he asked.

I turned to face him—a stout deputy holding a shotgun half at the ready.

"Evening," I said.

"You didn't answer my question, son."

I nodded my head toward the oak tree. "I'm headed over there. To investigate."

He cocked his head at me, wondering who I might be—someone he might throw out, or someone he dare not cross.

"I'm a reporter with the *Litchfield Ledger*," I said. "I'll show you my press card if you want."

He relaxed his posture and nodded.

I reached slowly for my wallet and showed him my card.

He snatched it, perused it briefly, and then handed it back, smiling. "Nelson Ingram. Well, goddamn, why didn't you say so? Your daddy saved my daddy's ass back in '57 when he got sued."

He put out his hand, "John Bernerd."

Despite my father's debilitating alcoholism and failed law practice, he had made a sizable impression on this community. Perhaps it was because the only thing that Southerners liked better than success was noble failure, and my father had come the closest to fitting this particular bill in recent memory. In any case, I was not loath to trade on this goodwill. I was the newly hired police and city desk reporter for the *Litchfield Ledger*, afternoon daily for all of Potter County and half of neighboring Colequit County, and I needed all the help I could get with the local authorities.

I shook his hand. "Pleased to meet you, John. What's going on over by the oak tree?"

He waved his hand in the direction of the tree and shook his head. "Some nigra boy. Strung up. Thought that was a thing of the past—but these days. . . ." His voice trailed off.

We both turned and walked toward the oak. He hung there in the glare of the headlights, a young black man, head wrenched back in the grip of the noose, chest naked, legs clothed in paint-spattered army fatigues, muddy hightops on his feet.

"Who the hell is this?" a hard voice demanded. Another shadow loomed before me in the dark.

Bernerd spoke for me. "Sheriff, this is Nelson Ingram. He's with the *Ledger*."

"How the hell did they get onto this so damn fast?" the sheriff snorted.

"Police scanner," I said. "It helps keep me on top of things."

I caught a glimpse of the name tag on his shirt: SHERIFF HAROLD STANTON. A tall man, Stanton stood ramrod straight in khakis that, despite the hour, looked immaculate and freshly pressed. He paused for an instant, digesting this bit of news dyspeptically. His eyes narrowed as he took the measure of me. He motioned for me to follow him.

"Kinda late to still be on the job," I said, walking with him. "Why don't you leave this to the night shift?"

"This is my county," he said. "I like to keep track of who's killing who."

He nodded toward the body. "Patrolman spotted him about half an hour ago. Been dead just a few hours from the look of him. Coroner's on his way now."

"Who would do this?" I asked, feigning incredulity.

"Hard to say. Don't know who he is. Could have had enemies. Could always be drugs."

"Drugs don't hang people."

He shrugged. "Who knows what people do these days." He said "people" with a certain inflection, meaning black people. I thought I could hear a clipped Cajun rhythm in his accent.

I let a moment of silence hang between us, then asked, "A young black man strung up—doesn't this have the look of, you know . . . the *Klan* about it?"

He snorted. "The Klan doesn't have a pot to piss in anymore in these parts. They got their ass whipped in a civil suit five years ago—court confiscated all their property. The best they can do these days is meet in Junior Cunningham's garage and swap Bull Conner stories."

"Junior Cunningham?"

"Bubba Cunningham's boy. Runs a body shop in town. Him and his buddies still carry the torch. Axe handles, Stars and Bars. You know the sort." He turned and spat.

"What better motive than misplaced revenge?"

He put his arm around my shoulder and walked me away from the oak tree. Flashbulbs began flaring one after another, fleeting blue strobes, as someone photographed the scene. "Believe me, Nelson, the Klan's just a tea and sympathy society around here nowadays."

A siren wailed closer now, and the ambulance came up over a rise and into view. I turned and faced the hanging body again.

"Who else would take the time and effort to do this? There are easier and safer ways to kill someone."

He pulled off his hat. "Folks is crazy these days. You can't figure 'em."

He turned and walked to the street to wave in the ambulance.

I got out a pad and began jotting down a few things—noting the details of the body. The hightops were British Knights and almost new. The mud staining them was still damp and a deep black-brown—quite different from the rust red clay on the ground. The fatigue pants were in a camouflage pattern and spattered with many different colors of paint. I walked up closer and peered at the legs as they dangled in front of me—mostly pastel colors, some glossy, some flat. Looked like house paints.

"Stand back!" someone yelled at me.

A pair of EMTs came with a litter from the ambulance. The body slowly settled to the ground in front of me as somebody lowered the rope from where it had been tied to the tree. It slumped stiffly to one side. I bent over the body. He had been a thin but well-muscled man, the chest without mark and hairless. Flashbulbs bloomed again as shutters clicked.

"Excuse us, sir," an EMT said and they both stooped and lifted the body onto their litter. One of them loosened the rope from around his neck. I winced, watching potential evidence wasted. They wheeled him away and loaded the litter into the ambulance. Another car had pulled up, and out of it came the coroner, Wade Bannister. He poked his head into the ambulance and nodded. He turned and spat.

"Dead," he said.

The coroner's office was an elective post and Wade was actually a retired accountant who ran for the job out of boredom and because all the physicians in the county were too busy. Most of Wade's qualifications came from his dedicated viewing of *Quincy* reruns. The pathologist at the local hospital performed the actual postmortems. Despite his lack of formal training, Wade had little trouble recognizing death when he saw it. The EMTs closed up the back doors of the ambulance and sped off, slinging gravel and letting the siren scream, even though their cargo could scarcely profit from their haste.

Wade stood around and chatted with the sheriff. I strolled out of the halo of headlights into the shadows past the oak tree. The ground back there settled gently into a low spot that was still muddy from this afternoon's storm. A wide arc of tire tracks traversed the mud, fresh and untainted by the tracks of other cars. I bent over them, but it was too dim to tell much—only that they were car or light truck tires. From the size of the wheelbase, they were tracks from a large car. They faded into the hardpack clay in the direction of the highway.

"Ingram!" Stanton yelled. "Quit fucking up the scene!" His voice trailed off as he came to stand beside me and saw the tire tracks. "Danny!" he called over his shoulder. "Get your ass over here!"

An officer ran up. Stanton gestured. "Get me photos and impressions of those. Why didn't you tell me we had a clean set of tracks back here?"

"Didn't see 'em," Danny said, and hustled back to a patrol car for more equipment.

The sheriff wrapped his arm around my shoulder and steered me back toward the highway. "Look here, Ingram. Why don't you leave all this to us."

"I'm just trying to gather a little information."

He sighed. "There'll be a full report in the morning in plenty of time for tomorrow's edition. Just leave the forensics to the pros."

I cringed, thinking of the multiple breaches they had already made in the investigation. He walked me to the shoulder of the highway and waited while I headed off toward my car.

I climbed into my car and drove back to the fish camp, reflecting that it was probably better to go along with things and keep good relations with the Powers-That-Be.

MY father's fish camp was an overgrown three-acre lot on the banks of the Sour Mash River. Its approach from the highway was marked only by a corroded aluminum gate that lay sprung from its hinges at the entrance to the front drive. A potholed dirt road led from the highway beneath a canopy of overhanging branches to the house, which stood at the side of the river raised up some twenty feet off the ground on telephone poles as protection against the spring floods. In the beam of my headlights at night the house seemed a foreboding silhouette suspended in the air beneath the branches.

I pulled the car in beside the house and ascended the rickety steps to the door. In the dark, I fumbled with the keys, opened the door, and went inside.

The damp musty air hung still and heavy, seemingly unchanged in thirty years. Standing at the threshold in the dark, I could remember the way it had been on any one of a hundred hunting and fishing weekends when I was a child. The heavy mildewed air, the smell of man-flesh confined in close warm spaces—tobacco and sweat and alcohol and Old Spice—the creak and snore of men slumped in the cots scattered across the living room and bedroom, deep in boozy sleep after a long day of shooting and drinking. I switched the light on and the living room lay before me, empty and silent.

I threw my keys onto the kitchen counter and went to the liquor cabinet to pour myself a whiskey. I fished a few ice cubes, well-water gray, from the freezer and plopped them into the drink. The water brought a strange sedimentary taste to the alcohol. I sipped at it and went out onto the screened porch that overlooked the river.

The Sour Mash flowed past, rippling in the moonlight, murmuring. The night had turned quiet, marked only by the throaty gurgling of the river frogs.

When I had returned to Litchfield, I had found the house locked tight. No one had crossed its threshold in years. Dust lay thick on the floors, mildew perfumed all the furniture and mattresses, cobwebs decorated every corner. I made a few cursory efforts at cleaning the place, but finally reconciled myself to its air of moldy dishevelment. Certainly I did not enjoy living here, but neither was I in any apparent hurry to leave. Poverty and lack of alternatives dictated my moving in. The sentimental and dreadful mixture of memories that the place engendered kept me there, unhappy but unable to leave, attracted and repulsed at the same time.

My father had purchased this property when I was a small boy. At that time it had been only a lot speckled with live oak and scrub pine amid runs of tall grass. I vaguely remember him taking my mother and me out to see it one Sunday, crashing his huge Oldsmobile through the thickets that overgrew the narrow access road. He stood on the bank of the river and described his plans for the place to my mother—a lodge for hunting and fishing. Nothing came of it for the longest of times. The lot lay unused, visited once or twice yearly for impromptu inspections and new rounds of planning. Finally, my father scraped together a small sum and had this cabin built—a two-bedroom shack up on stilts.

The weekends stolen away at this cabin had been precious to him, an escape from the quandaries of his life. He approached them with eagerness and sentimentality, the time so short that he packed it overfull with guests and excursions. Hunting and fishing buddies from town and the next county and two states away would converge on the cabin, all good middle-aged Southern men aching for release in emotional recapitulations of the acts of ancestors both real and imagined.

After he had died, most of his properties were sold off in the wake of my mother's collapse, but the cabin had been kept in the family, probably out of nostalgia and because the bottom land on which it was built had limited value. It was all that remained of my inheritance.

I sat in one of the weathered rockers on the screened porch. It was well past midnight, but the air still hung wet and warm about me. I pulled hard at the whiskey, unable to get the sight of that young man out of my mind. One drink led to a second, then a third. Then I stopped counting.

2

Wednesday Morning

MY alarm went off the next morning at its usual barbaric hour. I had taken to sleeping on a lounger on the screen porch, as the rest of the house was unbearably hot far into the night. The birds began their annoying chorus before dawn and the clock radio atop the refrigerator began squalling soon after.

Left to my own devices, I tended to stay awake into the early morning hours and sleep through noon. Holding down a job that required me to be routinely conscious before the sun rose did not sit well. I woke every morning resentfully. My head pounded, my joints ached, my eyes stung and grated in their sockets as I tried to wash out the grit of a night's sleep in the lukewarm water of my bathroom sink.

I stared at myself in the corroded mirror, squinting in

the hard light of the bathroom, and cursed another day when my innate genius would go unrecognized and I would be compelled to work for a living. A hot shower did little to ease my soul's plight, and afterward I dressed grumpily, choked down a cup of instant coffee, then set out for work.

The sun rose as I drove down the highway toward town, the air still tepid and wet. I was only half-awake, and my mind grappled sluggishly with my plans for the coming day. The paper had a 10 A.M. deadline. I headed for the sheriff's office as a first order of business. Their headquarters lay just outside the town line on old Highway 82. The building was a functional cinder-block cube on an acre of blacktop. I pulled into the parking lot and strode inside as if I knew what I was doing. The desk sergeant eyed me blankly as I walked up to him.

"Ingram with the *Ledger*," I said authoritatively. "What have you learned about the hanging last night?"

He sat forward and rustled through some papers on his desk. The tone of my voice seemed to command reply. I had learned many years back that the aura of authority was often more important than actual authority itself. The impression of power was all that was needed. He pulled a typed page from his stack and handed it to me.

It had the physical description of the victim, but little else.

"Haven't you identified the body yet?" I asked.

He looked at me suspiciously, but still replied, "Prints will go out to the FBI today. A family reported someone matching his description as missing this morning, but they haven't ID'd the body yet."

"What's the name of the missing person?"

He hedged and leaned away from me. "They haven't ID'd anyone yet. You don't want to go jumping to conclusions."

"Did they make an official missing persons report?"

"Well . . . yeah."

"Then it's a matter of public record. What's the name?" I demanded.

He smiled. "Well, now, they reported it to the Litchfield police, not to us. May be public record in Litchfield, but here it's a privileged law-enforcement communication."

I rolled my eyes. "Now, Sergeant, you know I can just drive into town and get the name from the police. Why be difficult?"

"Privileged communication," he said, smiling.

So much for the voice of authority. I quickly jotted down the information he had given me, then browsed the arrest log for any other remarkable crimes from the past day. Little was there aside from a couple of DWIs and a domestic violence arrest.

I checked my watch. Seven o'clock.

The sun had cleared the horizon. Standing in the parking lot, looking at the gray strip of state highway running past, I felt that dispensation, that blessedness felt by drunks and ne'er-do-wells who find themselves unaccountably sober and intact in these cleanly early morning hours. The air came cool and soothing into my nostrils, the blacktop, the trees, the far horizon seemed preternaturally real, as if I had never really seen them before. I was here, alive in a fresh, new world where I did not belong. My stomach grumbled and a splash of bile boiled up in the back of my throat. I trudged off to my car and drove the last few miles into town to check out the facts at the police station.

AT the Litchfield police station, the blotter told the tale. Reginald Copley, twenty-seven-year-old black male, resident of Banfield, reported missing since last night. Five-foot-eight inches tall, one hundred fifty-five pounds. I scribbled his address and name while Desk Sergeant Beatty stared at me over his morning's first cup of coffee.

"Where's the coroner keeping our victim?" I asked.

The desk sergeant eyed me biliously. "County hospital," he said finally. "In the morgue."

I nodded, thanked him, and left. I checked my watch. It was fifteen to eight. Two hours until deadline. I could run out to the address of my missing person, but any family that he had would have most likely all have gone to the hospital to identify the body. I climbed into my car and headed for the hospital, hoping to catch them there and perhaps get a word with the pathologist.

LITCHFIELD'S county hospital sat on the edge of a large residential neighborhood, beside I-65 running east to Tuscaloosa and west to Jackson, Mississippi. It was a respectable facility for a town of Litchfield's size—three stories with a large medical office building beside it.

I spent twenty minutes wandering the halls, trying to find the morgue without drawing undue attention to myself. At this I failed miserably. Hospitals do little for their public image by advertising where the morgue is located. Finally, I found the department of pathology. Inside was only a sleepy lab technician, fumbling through a stack of reports. I stood there until he looked up.

"I'm looking for the chief pathologist," I said, calling on my voice of authority again.

He stared at me uncomprehending for an instant.

"Well, we only got one pathologist," he said finally. "That's Dr. Hartley."

"And where might I find him?"

"He's down in the morgue doing the post on the guy got strung up last night."

"And how might I get there?" I asked brusquely.

He hesitated. "It's closed to the public."

"I'm Nelson Ingram," I said, as if that meant something. "I'm with the *Ledger*, we need the facts for today's edition."

He demurred and gave me directions.

After two or three false turns, I finally managed to find the morgue—a set of grimy metal doors at the end of a dank corridor in the hospital's subbasement. I knocked and went in.

I walked into bright fluorescent lights filling a room of clean white tile and stainless steel. In the center sat a large rectangular steel table upon which lay the naked body of a black man. He was flayed open from his pubic bone up to his shoulders with the standard Y-shaped incision used for autopsies, his viscera gleaming wetly in the overhead lights. The sweet heavy ferric smell of fresh blood hung in the air, mixing with the scent of antiseptics and tobacco.

A compact elderly man dressed in a white smock and a butcher's apron stood over the body, holding a loop of intestine in one hand and a scalpel in the other. Despite the setting, he looked strangely familiar.

"May I help you?" he asked in a whiskey-roughened but genteel accent.

I had seen more than a few autopsies during my years in Richmond, but the sight of them never failed to unsettle me. The throat tightens, the gorge rises, the eyes turn away then look back, appalled and fascinated.

"I'm Nelson Ingram," I said, finding my voice at last. "I'm with the *Ledger*. Are you Dr. Hartley?"

He nodded.

"I would shake your hand," he said, "but as you can see, I'm preoccupied."

"Ah—yes. In fact, this is what I came to see you about. I take it that this is the victim from last night?"

He nodded again.

"Did the family identify him as Reginald Copley?" I asked.

"Sadly, they did. So young he was, and with a wife and child," he said in an elegiac tone.

He mobilized the loop of bowel he was holding and tied a string tightly around it.

"No mystery about the cause of death, really, but I was going to give him the once-over to make sure there wasn't any more to it."

"Death by hanging, then?"

"Heavens no," Hartley said. "He was shot in the back of the head. Small-caliber weapon. Entry wound in the back of the head. Hollow-point round—did the requisite damage."

He indicated a macerated specimen sitting on the table beside him that I realized was a badly mangled brain. He had already done the craniotomy. Looking back at the corpse, I noticed now the large incision across the top of the skull.

"Then he was already dead when he was hung?"

"Most likely. Powder burns on the scalp. Close range."

"Find anything else?"

He shook his head. "Not much. Been dead awhile by the time he was found. Maybe six hours. Paint under the fingernails, but the family says he worked as a house-painter."

He stripped off his gloves and moved to a desk that sat behind a low partition. He lit a cigarette and made a note on a piece of paper.

"You wouldn't be any kin to old Lawyer Ingram?" he asked.

I nodded. "He was my father."

"I thought so." He smiled. "Little Nelson."

He rose and shook my hand—a small, supple hand, cool to the touch but with a firm grip.

"Perhaps you don't remember me. Seymour Hartley. I used to hunt with your father from time to time. He was a hell of a man."

"Thank you."

"It was a shame the way he died. A great loss to the community. He was not adequately appreciated in his time." He took another puff from his cigarette and set it in the ashtray on his desk.

"He was falling down drunk when he died," I said. "How could that be a loss to the community?"

Hartley shook his head ruefully. "He drank too much. No one denies that. He drank to relieve his frustrations. They were many and weighed upon him."

He took another drag at his cigarette and stubbed it out. Rising slowly, he turned to me.

"You're not a child anymore. You should know how he felt," he said, a tone of rebuke in his voice. He pulled on a clean pair of latex gloves and turned back to his work on the corpse.

"You knew my father well?" I asked.

"Passing well, I suppose. He was a private man, but we did have our moments together."

"Out at the river cabin?" I asked.

"Yes," he said, smiling distantly. "There were more than a few weekends out there that I still remember fondly." He delved elbow deep into the viscera of the man's open belly.

I watched him work and came up with a fragment of a memory—a much younger, brown-haired version of this elderly man. I had a vision of him in a hunting vest leaning over the open hood of a pickup truck with my father. My father was happy leaning there with him over the warm radiator, the oily valve covers and open carburetor throat, existence boiled down to these simple things.

"You were 'Doc,' " I said.

"Excuse me?" he said.

"That's what they called you back then. When you were hunting with my father."

He smiled. "Yes. Always hated that."

I looked at my watch—eight forty-five. My deadline was fast approaching. "Do you have the victim's personal effects here?" I asked.

He inclined his head toward the cardboard box that lay in the corner.

"May I look through them?" I asked, opening the box.

"It's police property," he said, in a halfhearted protest. "Physical evidence. They won't appreciate your fiddling with it."

"I'll be gentle," I said.

The khaki fatigue pants lay on top, crusted with paint spatters. Underneath were the British Knights—black and white leather hightops with dark mud thick on the soles. The mud caked the soles, but also flowed up and covered the heels halfway up.

"He was killed somewhere else then brought to the place where he was hung," I said aloud as the idea came to me.

Dr. Hartley looked over from his work at the autopsy table. "What, son?"

"He was killed somewhere else, then dragged. His shoes are caked with this black mud—caked up the back of the heels as it would if he had been pulled face up with his heels dragging. The place where he was found was nothing but red clay. They killed him somewhere else, dragged him away, drove him to the scene, and strung him up."

"I take it that you've been doing this sort of work for some time."

I nodded. "I've got to run to make deadline. Mind if I call later for the full autopsy report?"

"That would be fine," he said. "Perhaps someday I can tell you more about your father—it might improve your opinion of him."

"I'd like that," I said, turning toward the door.

He smiled and nodded, brandishing a violaceous kidney in one hand as he turned toward a scale to weigh it.

3

Wednesday Morning

THE *Litchfield Ledger* building lay a half-block beyond the town hall, just off the courthouse square. It was a two-story, blunt-faced warehouse. The presses sat on the ground floor, and entering the front door, one was struck by the smell of machine oil and printer's ink. The presses droned and clattered, churning out the advertisements for tomorrow's edition. A right turn brought you to the stairwell and up into the editorial office. It was a large open room graced by large bays of windows on three of its walls, lending an airy light to an otherwise chaotic room. Desks and filing cabinets were arranged in a half-random fashion. In the far corner, partitioned off, sat Leyland Parish's office—the editor and publisher. From across the room I could see him hunched over his desk, washed in the faint glow of his computer—a late and grudging concession to modernity on his part. He glanced up at my arrival, harried and distracted, returning quickly to peck at the keyboard.

I made my way to my desk, sunk in a corner behind a row of filing cabinets. The cabinets guarded my left flank, and I could sit with my back to the wall and see the door to the stairwell off to my right. I was secure with all the approaches covered. Slinging my coat on the back of the chair, I sat down and riffled through the mat of papers that decorated my desktop.

I switched on the computer at my desk, lay my notes beside it, and set to work. Within thirty minutes I had a reasonable version of the facts assembled. I rewrote once, double-checked the spelling of all the names, then stored it, printed a hard copy, and sent a copy to Leyland. In the last twenty minutes I hashed out the arrest and accident reports.

Leyland walked up to my desk. "You on this lynching?" he asked.

He was a great wreck of a man, three hundred pounds draped in wrinkled seersucker, somewhere on the high side of sixty years old. His voice was classic elder-Alabama—thick and only half-enunciated, the words stirred like molasses at the back of the throat. The lips and jaw barely move, the sounds half-swallowed, emerging as gutturals with the barest shape of meaning. Thirty years before, Leyland would have spoken up closer to the front of his mouth, the words heavily accented and drawn-out, but nevertheless understandable. But with the passage of years and the accumulation of layers of respectability and authority, the voice thickens and slows, the sound settles in the back of the throat and emerges in rounded, deep protosyllables, heavy with import but dense and impenetrable to the untrained ear. As a native growing up here, one does not notice, as one fails to notice the poignant slanting light of a Southern sunset late in autumn. Returning here to the Deep South after two decades in voluntary exile, I found the accents alive—at once foreign and familiar, comprehensible yet as alien as Provençal French.

"Yessir," I said. "First story's been written. Turns out he was shot in the back of the head. They only lynched him for show."

"You got a name yet?"

"Reginald Copley—a housepainter, lived out in Banfield."

Leyland raised an eyebrow. "Not a bad morning's work," he said. He turned to head toward his office.

"Leyland?"

He turned back and regarded me with his baggy eyes.

I hesitated, suddenly unsure if I really wanted to broach this topic, "Do you think the Klan might have had a hand in this?"

He laid his eyes upon me and settled them there for a moment. He did not trust me by a long shot. I am sure he had so far found my copy competent but underwhelming.

"Why would you think that?"

"What's the motive otherwise?"

"Don't know enough to speak to motive," he said. "Don't start jumping to conclusions."

He turned and walked to his office. Halfway there he turned around and called to me, "Jaycees are having their monthly meeting today at the Holiday Inn. Make sure you cover it."

I bit my tongue hard. With a résumé that included work for the *L.A. Times* foreign desk, the *Cleveland Plain Dealer*'s city desk, and the *Richmond Times-Dispatch*'s police beat, I did not take easily to bending and scraping and such pissant assignments rankled.

In truth, I had little reason to expect better. At thirty-nine, the trail of my journalistic career stretched out behind me like the fiery wake of a meteor engaged in its inevitable descent. I had lost every newspaper job I had ever gotten, and in between had long years of time strangely unaccounted for in my résumé. Also unlisted were one divorce, a half-dozen failed relationships, and the squandering of a modest inheritance.

I had graduated from Princeton in 1970, never intending a career in journalism. My father's will had stipulated that I graduate from a reputable college before receiving my inheritance, no doubt in the hope that four years at a liberal arts institution would educate some of the Ingram fecklessness out of me. "Fond hope, Father!" I thought at the time as I decamped for points abroad, money in hand. I made the requisite tour of Europe, habituating the cafés of Paris, the bodegas of Spain, the atmospheric villages of Greece and Italy. After frittering away a few years, I settled in Venice with an ardent Italian girl. She was a Marxist and painfully serious. For a time, love blossomed. But after six months, her patience with me had begun to grow thin. In an effort to revive the relationship, we took a trip to Istanbul. This was quaint foreign travel even for an Italian girl, and briefly the relationship steadied.

Within a month, however, she had left me for a charismatic activist in Istanbul.

I returned to Venice adrift. A friend who was a stringer for Reuters suggested that I put together an article about Turkish politics. In a stroke of luck, just as I completed an impressionistic essay on the Turkish Communist Party, a leftist coup was foiled. Reuters snatched up my article. Soon after came a telegram from the *L.A. Times* soliciting copy. A series of pieces about the fate of the left in Turkey followed, each one more speculative as my material ran thin. After a while the copy began going unpublished. The paychecks slowed, then stopped.

My funds nearly exhausted, I finally returned to America and lied my way into a job with the *Cleveland Plain Dealer*. I suddenly found myself facing a daily deadline in a rude Northern town with packs of snarling Yankees and bloodless Midwesterners. In a year and a half I became a better reporter, but at the expense of too many deadlines missed, too many assignments botched. My editor, however, allowed me to resign quietly and even wrote me a letter of recommendation, which helped land my last real job—police reporter for the *Richmond Times-Dispatch*.

I did respectable work after a breaking-in period. How often it is, however, that a man's private life undoes him just as his professional life is achieving some order. I entered into an injudicious marriage. Mary Katherine McKluskey was her name—Mary Kate to all close to her. She was raven-haired, blue-eyed, fiery, painfully Irish, and the publisher's granddaughter.

While I had intended to make her a good and loyal

husband, I was sadly weak of flesh. Temptation came too often my way, and too often I proved unequal to the challenge. Fiery in love, she was terrible in rejection. After the first liaison was discovered I spent six months in private and professional disrepute. After many apologies, she took me back. I enjoyed another few months of favor, until I sinned and was caught again. I was thrown out, this time to stay. In a month the divorce terms were cut; six months later they were final.

My star, already dim at the paper, flamed out altogether. I was demoted to the society pages, then after a few months fired. At thirty-four, I was without job or prospects. I scared up a series of small-town jobs that I promptly lost, moving in a fog of alcohol. Quart bottles of whiskey dissolved in my presence.

Several years passed in this way. Finally, three months past my last job, I found myself playing out the tag ends of a college chum's hospitality at a Key West condo, sitting watching the surf pound the beach, deep into a bottle of rum with a .357 in my lap, contemplating pulling the trigger—an act any Ingram could feel a mystical pull toward. I even held the gun to my head and clicked the hammer onto an empty chamber. I threw the gun into a corner, hoping that my host would wait a few more days before sending me on my way.

I had not to wait a few more days, however, for the next morning I received the call from my Uncle Rayburn telling me to come as soon as possible to attend my mother's funeral.

4

Wednesday Morning

THE stretch of road that separated Litchfield from Banfield was dreary beyond the norm for this part of Alabama. Scrub oaks and stands of pine flanked the road, punctuated by tin-roofed shacks with the broken hulks of autos and tractors sitting in the yards. Weeds crowded the shoulders of the road, sharing the space with empty bottles and windblown trash.

Banfield itself was little more than a post office and a minute mart on either side of the highway. Not even a stoplight marked the encounter between town and motorist; a transient drop in the speed limit was all that distinguished the meeting. It was a receding speck in the rearview mirror before one had even noticed it.

I pulled into the minute mart and got out to ask directions. A thin young black girl stood at the cash register wearing an Atlanta Braves cap and a baggy sweatshirt. She eyed me suspiciously as I approached.

"Excuse me," I said, showing her the address in my notebook. "Can you tell me how to get to the Copley house?"

She looked from me to the notebook and back again. "Who want to know?" she asked finally.

I smiled disarmingly. "I'm with the *Ledger*," I said. "I just want to talk with the family."

She eyed me warily, then leaned over the counter to look out to the parking lot, saw my junk heap of a car, then turned back to me, smiling. "The Man don't drive in that car," she laughed then gave me directions.

I walked out to my car. I guess the old heap gave me some cachet. It was a battered, rusty, fifteen-year-old white Ford LTD that Uncle Rayburn had loaned me after my return. Underneath the hood lay a monstrous V-8 that was capable of impressive feats of acceleration. Rayburn had nicknamed it "Hubert," after the late vice-president and senator from Minnesota, explaining that, like Hubert, the car was "white and not worth a damn."

THE town of Banfield was a few hundred homes and shacks scattered across a couple of dozen square miles of woods and overgrown fields. Throughout the South there must have been hundreds of towns like this—unincorporated, disenfranchised collections of frame houses, shotgun shacks, and corroded trailers distinguished in the records of government often by only a zip code.

With the collapse of the plantation system after the

Civil War, many blacks had drifted to the cities of the North, but others remained behind and eked out a living as sharecroppers, tied to the land by debt and poverty just as effectively as they had been bound by slavery. The civil rights movement may have broken down many of the more visible barriers of segregation but a moribund economy and exhausted farmland combined to keep rural blacks poor and marginalized. Johnson's Great Society brought some improvements, but only enough to perpetuate a helpless poverty. The economic boom of the sixties never came to Potter County, while the inflation of the seventies and the recessions and social cutbacks of the eighties did. Conditions now were little different from how they had been a hundred years ago. Electricity had still not made it to many of the homes. Half of them did not have indoor plumbing. Most of them did not have heat in the winter beyond woodstoves.

In other ways things were not as bad as what I had seen in the ghettos of Cleveland. There was little crime, no pollution, wide-open spaces. But what made it worse was the sense of its permanence here, the feeling that everyone accepted it. In the bad parts of Cleveland or Richmond there was at least an air of outrage and anger that suggested some possibility for change or escape. But here there was only a silence and denial that was generations old. Outrage was a stranger, anger a fugitive. I shook my head. Outrage was a luxury I could not afford either. As a reporter I could not take sides without losing whatever thin credibility I had. Besides, it would have been like shaking a fist at the stars in a land where everyone pretended it was always daytime.

I drove down dirt roads, leaving a cumulus of dust behind me, holding my scribbled directions in one hand while I steered with the other, peering over the wheel for obscure landmarks—left at the live oak past the creek gully, right at the rusty schoolbus parked in the churchyard. Chickens pecked in the dirt at the shoulder of the road and followed my passing with beaded gaze. I turned down a rutted dirt road flanked on either side with a split-rail fence. An old black man leaned against the fence and watched my approach.

I pulled onto the shoulder beside him. He stared at me, muddy brown eyes looking out of deep sockets in an ancient weathered face. His jaws worked on a chaw of tobacco.

I leaned out my open window. "Excuse me," I said, "is this the way to the Copley house?"

He eyed me impassively, as he might regard a museum specimen—"Crazy White Man Lost in the Backwoods." He turned his head and spat a brown stream of spittle into the ground near my car's front tire, then turned back to stare at me with his magisterial reserve.

"I'm with the newspaper," I said. "I just want to talk to his family."

He focused his eyes on me a little more directly as I spoke to him, then looked at my wreck of a car. He smiled. It seemed that Hubert's dilapidation was reassurance to all that I wasn't some kind of undercover cop.

With infinite deliberation he lifted an arm and gestured down the road in the direction I was headed.

"Shoah," he said in a voice thick and deep with a backwoods Alabama dialect. He went on to give me directions that I could understand only after reflection and translation: "Go down a half-mile, then turn left. Second house on the left."

I nodded my thanks and pulled back out onto the road. A half-mile later I turned onto a narrow, barely visible track—no more than a pair of wheel ruts across a grassy field. A triplet of one-story houses sat back off the road among the trees. The yard of the middle house was full of cars, people clustered on the porch and in the side yard by the kitchen door. I parked and got out.

Heads turned toward me; eyes followed me as I walked toward the house. It was a square clapboard house with an ample front porch. A sea of black faces stood on it and watched my hesitant approach.

"Morning," I called out.

A few of the men nodded, then looked away. I came to the steps to the porch. The crowd parted, clearing a path to the front door for me.

"Is this the Copley home?" I asked.

A bald fireplug of a man jerked his chin down and stood half in my way. "Yes, it is. And who might you be?" His voice was deep and stentorian. I figured him for a preacher.

"I'm with the *Litchfield Ledger*," I said, and stepped up onto the porch. I reached to shake his hand. He took my hand reluctantly. "Ingram," I said, "Nelson Ingram."

"Come in, Mr. Ingram," he said gravely, shaking my hand. "The family is inside."

I pulled open the screen door and went inside. Again a sea of black faces turned toward me as I entered.

"Good morning," I said.

A stout small black woman dressed in a black dress sitting on the sofa in the front room straightened up to full height and replied, "Good morning."

From her air of command, I figured her for the victim's mother.

"Sorry to bother you, ma'am," I said. "I'm Nelson Ingram with the *Litchfield Ledger*. I wonder if I could ask you a few questions."

"Mr. Ingram," she said, looking around the room, "my son has been killed." Her eyes misted and she looked down. She gathered herself. "Could you come back later—tomorrow?"

"Mrs. Copley," I said, and looked at the assembled group searching for support, "I know your son has been killed. I was there when he was found."

A murmur filled the room.

"I saw what was done to him. I'm just here looking for answers. I don't know who did this. But if I can learn something about him, maybe I can help to find out."

She stared at me a long moment.

"Very well, Mr. Ingram," she said and rose slowly and turned toward the kitchen. "Come with me."

I went to her side. She took my arm and we walked into the kitchen. There was another group of people standing around the kitchen table, talking quietly. Mrs. Copley turned to them. "Please," she said, "give me a few minutes to talk with Mr. Ingram alone."

People sifted quietly out to the front room. She gestured toward the kitchen table. "Please be seated, Mr. Ingram."

It was an ancient table, chrome-plated metal tubing

for legs, a worn piece of Formica for its top. We sat in mismatched chairs opposite each other. She was a small plump woman, dark-skinned with a full generous face creased with age and worry. She peered at me through wide-framed thick bifocals, nut-brown eyes red from crying magnified behind the lenses. She wore a black dress with a high black lace collar. A black wig sat atop her head like an inverted bird's nest, barely covering her gray hair.

Worrying a handkerchief between her fingers, she asked, "What can I tell you, Mr. Ingram?"

"Tell me about your son."

"He was a good boy, Mr. Ingram. He didn't cause me trouble. He had just been married to a girl he met out West. They have a little baby." She looked down and cleared her throat. "He had a job, worked every day painting houses. Never missed a day."

"Who did he work for?"

"A contractor in Litchfield—Mr. Jimmy Anderson. Reginald liked the work and was doing good at it." She put her head in her hands and began to cry softly.

"Reggie was a *good* boy," she said. "He wasn't into no trouble."

A commotion came from the front room, a shrill voice cut through our words, and a young black woman stormed into the kitchen.

"Are you the reporter?" she asked.

Her voice was flat and generic, without color, speaking of lost occidental desert places like California. She stared directly at me, eyes smoldering—beautiful deep brown almond-shaped eyes set in a smooth, light-skinned face with full lips and a delicately flared nose.

Dressed in a short-cut black dress, she leaned over me like an avenging angel. For a moment, I was overcome.

"Latoya, please!" Mrs. Copley said in a voice of command. The girl flashed her an angry look, but said nothing.

"Yes," I said, finding my wits again, "I'm the reporter."

I stood and turned to face her.

"Nelson Ingram," I said in as courtly a fashion as I could muster. "With the *Litchfield Ledger*."

Mrs. Copley stood as well. "This is Reggie's wife," she said, "Latoya Copley."

With her face turned away, she cut her eyes up at me—eyes burning with anger. She pursed her lips bitterly. "Who killed my Reggie?" she said in a hushed voice, the words bitten off and spat at me.

"I don't know. I wish I did. Do you know who would want to?"

She looked away. A presence filled the doorway behind her—a tall muscular black man, six-four, shaved skull, and goatee, an earring dangling from one ear.

"Who is this honky?" he asked.

The usage was dated and the accent a generic Western one, as Latoya's was. He pushed past her into the kitchen toward me, looming. He was not a young man, perhaps in his late thirties. He exuded an air of violence, dull malevolent eyes fixing me with an indifferent hostility, as one might regard a roach before it was crushed.

"Malcolm—" Mrs. Copley said, but he cut her off.

"Who is this honky?" he repeated.

He stood mere inches away. I attempted an air of

calm. "I'm with the *Ledger*," I said, "investigating Reginald Copley's death."

"We don't need you here," he said, his voice quiet and precise.

"Malcolm!" Mrs. Copley shouted again.

"Hush, Auntie," Malcolm said, cutting his eyes at her. She demurred and sat back down.

I did a silent double take at this exchange and turned to stare intently at Malcolm. In the South few had the supremacy of the elderly black matriarch. By comparison, white women paled into irrelevance, exerting what power they had only through guile and intrigue. Black grandmothers usually sat at the hub of large extended families, ruling with iron determination and brooking no back talk. No black man would usually dare question her authority even in private, much less with company, and never in the presence of white folk. Who was this Malcolm to defy her so openly and have her so openly retreat?

"You need to leave now, Mr. Reporter," he said, again quietly.

I looked from him to Mrs. Copley. She looked away, worrying her handkerchief.

"Perhaps you best leave," she said.

I nodded and turned to the kitchen door. Malcolm barred my path and refused to move.

"Excuse me," I said, and edged around him toward the doorway. I felt Latoya's eyes on me and turned to look at her. She fixed me with her gaze.

"You find who killed him," she said.

Malcolm shoved her. "Shut up," he said, then turned to me. "You just stay out of it, white boy."

I walked out the doorway and into the front room to be greeted by a silent roomful of faces. As I moved toward the front door, they all looked away. I heard a baby's cry from a back room.

On the front porch the crowd still stood. They watched silently as I made my way down the steps and across the yard. I checked my watch—eleven-thirty.

I started the car and headed back the way I had come. I saw a figure running toward my car from off to the right, waving me down. It was Latoya. She leaned into my open window. Again her beauty, her fiery almond eyes, took me aback.

"You find the men who killed Reggie," she said, her anger palpable.

"Do you know who they might be?"

"I don't know, but you find them."

"Who's this Malcolm?"

"Malcolm—" She turned and looked back toward the house to check that she wasn't being watched. "Malcolm's crazy. Don't mess with him."

"But who is he?" I asked.

"Nobody. Just a crazy nigger." She looked back toward the house again. "I gotta go," she said, and as quickly was gone, loping back across the front yard in long graceful strides.

I sat for a moment in my car, marveling at her. She was like a thorny rose amid this field of dandelions. This place needed more of her anger.

5

Wednesday Afternoon

I DROVE from Banfield back to Litchfield and searched out Junior Cunningham's body and fender shop. Junior was the oldest of Bubba Cunningham's sons. Now deceased, Bubba had been the Grand Dragon of the Potter County chapter of the Ku Klux Klan. Junior had inherited his father's politics, if not his organizational assets. If hate crimes were the topic, Junior had best be on the short list.

The body shop occupied a corner lot in the backstreets of Litchfield near the train tracks. Wrecked and dented cars littered the property, scattered around a dingy garage with a lift and a pair of grease pits. The hand-painted sign atop the building read CUNNINGHAM'S BODY AND FENDER with a pair of rebel flags on either side of the lettering.

The garage was cacophonous with the sound of disc sanders and hammers. The smell of burnt metal and fresh primer filled the room. Junior sat behind a desk in the back of the garage. He was a large, potbellied man in his late fifties, a crew cut perched above a broad face that had gone jowly with the advance of years. The desk was cluttered with stacks of invoices and papers. On the wall behind him hung a well-polished ax handle and a *Snap-On* cheesecake calendar. As I walked toward him, he looked up.

"Morning," he said, his voice nasal, the word drawn out then bitten off in the front of his mouth.

I nodded, replying, "Nice day, ain't it?"

"Guess so. What can I do for you?"

"Got a Datsun pickup with a dented front quarter-panel," I said. "What'd it cost to get a new one with matched paint?"

He rocked back in his desk chair. "Depends," he said. "Can't predict spare parts."

"Ballpark estimate," I said.

"Depends," he said. "Two, three hundred. Who knows."

"Why don't I bring it by tomorrow," I said. "Let you take a look."

He nodded. "Anytime."

"What'd you think about that nigra boy they strung up?" I asked as casually as I could.

He narrowed his eyes and rocked forward in his chair. "What's it to ya?"

I shrugged. "Nothing much. Just ain't something you see much anymore, that's all."

He kept his squinted gaze fixed on me. "Don't know nothin' about it," he said.

I sat down in the chair opposite him. The staccato bark of an impact wrench split the air for an instant, then the normal background din of the garage returned.

"I know you don't know nothin'," I said. "It's just that it reminds me of . . . other times."

He leaned forward and hissed through clenched teeth, "Who the fuck are you?"

I smiled and looked him in the eyes. "No one," I said. "A concerned citizen. That's all."

"That's touching," he said. "That's real touching. I think it's time for you to leave." He nodded toward the door.

"I just wanted to see if Dixie was worth a goddamn anymore," I said, giving my Southern drawl full rein, and turned to leave.

He came across the desk, grabbed my arm, and pulled me close.

"Listen to me," he said in a half-whisper. "I ain't shedding no tears over that colored boy, but *we* don't do that kind of thing anymore. You catch my drift? I don't know who the fuck you are—FBI or ACLU or just some nosy do-gooder—but you can just start looking for someone else to pin this one on."

I smiled and held my hands out to my sides, showing my open palms.

"No trouble, brother. Just making a little conversation."

He let me go and sat back down, wiping back his crew cut.

"Whatever. Those days are done. I don't know who

hung that little motherfucker, but I'm not losing any sleep over it."

"When can I bring the truck in?" I asked.

"There ain't no fucking truck," he said, eyeing me evenly. "Now get." And he gestured again toward the door.

"The old days are gone?" I asked.

"Long gone," he said.

"Where?"

"Into the pockets of fat-ass lawyers, that's where. Twenty years ago, we had money and a meeting hall out in the county near the river, then some fat-ass ACLU lawyer broke our backs in civil court on some damn nuisance suit—took every dime the local chapter had, drove away the membership. If it'd been a fat-ass liberal lawyer found strung up, then maybe you'd have cause to come nosing around here. . . . Shit, it's all gone," he said, and shook his head.

I dared not tell him that it was my father who first got the civil suit in process that years later culminated in the judgment that broke the local Klan. I nodded my thanks and left.

I had the Jaycees luncheon still to attend. The morning's cool had long since gone, replaced by a sweltering heat. The sun marched up the sky, the air grew wet and heavy, and cumulus clouds blossomed high into the stratosphere.

THE Jaycees met in the conference room of the Holiday Inn, which lay at the outskirts of the town beside the Interstate. I pulled my car into the parking lot, loosening my collar against the heat. The blacktop radiated like a griddle; my shirt hung limply on me, already damp with sweat.

The Holiday Inn was cool and dim inside, exuding the carpeted vinyl sameness that comforted weary travelers from coast to coast. Getting into the luncheon took a little doing, but finally I convinced them that I was with the honorable press. I was actually interested to hear if there was any talk about the lynching.

The conference room was a square space with a low acoustic ceiling. Dining tables were scattered across its expanse, a dais with a small lectern at the end of the room opposite the doors. The hubbub of voices and the clatter of flatware against china filled the room. Young white businessmen bent over plates of fried chicken, collards, and okra. The only black faces I could see belonged to the waiters and busboys. I found a chair along the wall in the back and tried to tune my ears to the conversations at the adjacent few tables.

College football, specifically the prospects for the Crimson Tide in the upcoming season, dominated the talk at the nearest table. Although it was only June, this was a topic that rarely failed to excite. The sager among them chewed their chicken and grumbled knowingly about the decline of standards since the passing of The Bear. A few talked optimistically about new prospects and intimated inside information on the coaching and personnel changes that were to make the difference this year.

I shuddered a little inwardly. Looking at this room of earnest young white businessmen, hustling this deal and that in their restrained middle-of-the-day murmuring drawls, I thought, there but for the grace of God go I. For good or bad, four years at Princeton, wandering in Europe, and exile in the rude North had spoiled me for such a life. I wondered if perhaps I'd have been happier if I had gone to Tuscaloosa or Auburn, majored in business, and come back to Litchfield to press the flesh with these good old boys, paying homage to the Holy Southern Trinity of Church, Business, and Football.

Someone up at the dais rapped a gavel. A plump middle-aged man in a polyester suit stood at the lectern and tapped at the microphone.

"Let's get goin', folks," he said.

The murmured conversation slowly died down as the speaker went on. "Welcome to the monthly Jaycee's luncheon. We're glad to have y'all. I'd like to go through the minutes of the last meeting."

He riffled through a stack of papers and began to drone out a litany of motions, activities and fund-raising events, votes taken, committees organized. I jotted all this down furiously, for these were the little facts that readers wanted to see duly noted in the *Ledger*. Eventually the speaker finished and cleared his throat.

"I'd now like to introduce our speaker this afternoon," he went on. "He's one of the key figures behind the GreenDowns Dog Track that has brought a much-needed boost to our community. He's a local boy, been up North for a few years, and now come back to help us out. Gentleman, welcome Riley Hill," he said and gestured to the man seated at his right.

A smattering of applause greeted the speaker as he rose to the podium.

"Thank you," he said in Deep Southern, nodding and smiling.

Riley Hill was a thick-necked, rotund man somewhere past fifty. Short black hair hung lankly, a lock combed over a growing bald spot. A couple of extra chins hung over his button-down collar. He fiddled with the microphone and fidgeted as he pulled out a set of notes from a coat pocket and shuffled them in a pair of beefy hands.

"I want to thank y'all for asking me here today," he said. "I'm proud to be here and proud to be part of new business ventures here in the New South."

This was an applause line, and the audience responded feebly.

He nodded and grunted little Elvis "thank-you's" into the mike. He entered into his prepared remarks, a monotonous speech about the booming opportunities in the South, sprinkled with commonplace praise and homage to Southern virtue and industry. I scratched out the bare outlines of the talk, trusting that I could improvise the rest if I needed it for the newspaper.

As the talk wandered on, I caught the soft undercurrent of conversation picking up again at the nearby tables. I thought I heard the words "nigra" and "lynching" in the murmured talk, but could not make out the sense of the conversation. I pricked my ears while pretending to concentrate on the speaker. Two men had kicked back from their table and sat shoulder to shoulder, jaw to jaw, talking in hushed voices. I strained but could make out nothing more, except a disdainful murmur. Then the words were swallowed up altogether in another round of applause.

Riley Hill drew to a close, and this was greeted with more meek applause as he folded up his notes and sat down. The moderator thanked him and made a few brief announcements then moved on to new business. Chairs scraped backward from the tables as a few people rose to leave early. I followed close on the trail of the two whose conversation I had overheard. They still hewed to their topic, and I gathered from the thrust of their remarks that neither of them mourned Reginald Copley's passing.

"Reckon he had it coming?" I asked, pressing in from behind them.

They regarded me from over their shoulders skeptically. "I reckon he probably did," one of them said finally.

"Usually do when you get lynched," the other said wryly. "Y'know we ain't allowed to hang 'em for sport no more." They both guffawed and walked off together.

6

Wednesday Afternoon

JIMMY Anderson's contracting business was an office front two blocks off the Courthouse Square, just a block from the offices of the *Ledger*. His secretary was the only one in the office. She told me that Jimmy was out on a job on the lake, and gave me the address.

Lake Litchfield was really little more than the dammed southern end of the Sour Mash River, a sinuous twenty-mile ribbon of a lake, already silting up although it was only ten years old. The original rationale for the lake was as a reservoir for the county, but it was also approved for recreation, and its shores were becoming packed with expensive homes with docks and boathouses for the well-to-do of Litchfield and Tuscaloosa. My father's river cabin was many miles north of the dam, where the river was still just a narrow span good for only fishing.

Jimmy Anderson was out with his crew on one of the new developments along the lake. I drove over a freshly paved asphalt road through a stand of new growth to the construction site, a set of four houses on a clear spot in a bend in the lake. The air felt lighter in this large open space. The blue dome of the sky was filled with pillars of gray-white cumulus clouds, marching up from the south like bulls. A skilsaw began screaming from the nearest house, a keening sound that dropped in pitch as the saw bit into the wood.

A man with a proprietary air about him sat at a card table under a lean-to, looking over blueprints. He did not look up as I approached.

"Afternoon," I said. "Mr. Anderson?"

Still he did not look up. "What can I do for you?"

"I'm with the *Litchfield Ledger*—Nelson Ingram," I said. "I'm looking for information about Reginald Copley."

He glanced up at me, regarding me from behind RayBan sunglasses. "What about him?" he asked.

I shrugged nonchalantly. "I don't know. What was he like as an employee? Was he responsible, on time, dependable?"

He shrugged in reply. "He was all right. Showed up and gave me a good day's work. Until today. Didn't show up this morning. What do you want with him?"

"Didn't you know?" I asked. "He was murdered last night. Strung up."

He raised his sunglasses. "That so?" he said, seemingly surprised.

I nodded.

He shook his head ruefully.

"Any reason anyone would want to do that to him?" I asked.

"I don't know much about these boys, but he got along real well on the job. No trouble."

"Was he at work the day he was killed?"

He thought for a moment. "Yesterday? Yeah, showed up on time, worked a full day."

"Anything different about yesterday?"

"We knocked off a little early because of the thunderstorm. About four-thirty."

"Who'd he leave with?"

"I don't know. He usually comes with Bennie."

"Bennie?"

"Yeah, one of the colored boys," he said, waving dismissively. "He's working over at the second house there."

I thanked him, turned, and hiked across the lot, picking my way among the scattered scrap wood, piles of gravel, and construction site trash. Stepping over a roof truss lying next to the foundation, I climbed up into the half-framed house. Bennie stood shirtless in the rafters of the house, driving nails with a nail gun in a staccato rhythm, a slim young black man in blue jeans, sweating in the afternoon sun. I stood on the first floor, staring up at him as he worked. After awhile he looked down at me. I waved. He nodded and paused.

"Afternoon," I said, nodding affably.

He stared at me, then looked around for a moment, as if checking to see if anyone was watching. Finally, he returned my greeting, put down the nail gun, then dropped softly from the rafters to the flooring beside me.

"I'm Nelson Ingram," I said, holding out my hand. "I'm with the *Ledger*. I understand you knew Reginald Copley."

"Yeah," he said, eyeing me warily, "I knew him."

"You've heard what happened to him?"

He nodded. "Yeah," he said sadly.

"I wonder if I could ask you a few questions about him?"

"Sure," he said, still staring at me closely. "We drove to work together every day. We were tight." He did not have the thick, languorous dialect of a country black, but instead talked with the more smoothed-out accent of a city dweller.

"Who would want to kill him?"

He looked down and away. "I don't know, man. That's the thing—Reggie didn't have any enemies. Everyone liked him."

"Did he go out much at night? Did he like to party?"

He shook his head. "No—not Reggie. He just got married, got a kid. He pretty much stayed home nights."

"Pretty much of a family man?"

"Yeah, he'd pretty much settled down."

"I'll bet he was hell in his younger days," I said with a conspiratorial laugh.

Bennie laughed in return. "Yeah! Reggie and me—we used to raise some righteous hell back when we ran together in Birmingham." He laughed again. "Man, we had raised some righteous hell!"

"Just kid's stuff?"

"I guess you could call it that. Later he moved out to California and I went into the service."

"How'd you both end up in a godforsaken place like Litchfield?"

He smiled, acknowledging the incongruity. "Reggie's momma got sick and she moved back here to be with her people. Reggie came back to be with her. He got this construction job and called me up in Birmingham. I wasn't doing nothing, and they needed skilled people so I came here for the work."

"Reggie ever do any civil rights work—even out in California?"

He looked at me quizzically for a moment then shook his head. "No, man. That wasn't his thing. Live and let live—that was him. He didn't stir things up."

Silence hung between us for a moment.

"Who's this Malcolm hanging around his house?" I asked finally.

Bennie's eyes cut up toward me then rapidly away. "He's Reggie's brother-in-law—from California. Latoya's brother."

"What's he doing here in Alabama?"

"Nothing. Just hanging out, sponging off them. That's all. Listen, I gotta get back to work."

"When was the last time you saw Reggie?"

"Yesterday. Right after work. I had just dropped him off on the turn to his house. He always liked to get out and walk from the highway to his house."

"Anything different about yesterday?"

He shook his head. "Not really."

"Anything at all?"

He thought for a long moment. "Well, I did see this

new car—a big, black sedan—come towards us as I was leaving. I remember watching it in my rearview as I pulled away."

"A big car?"

"Yeah, like a Towncar or a Caddy—you know, a big car."

"Notice the plates?"

He shook his head after a moment's contemplation.

Someone called to us from across the work site.

"I gotta get back to work," he said.

I thanked him and got his phone number. We shook hands. He turned and began climbing up a ladder.

"Reggie ever do drugs?" I asked.

He stopped and looked back at me. "No, man. Not anymore."

He shook his head, then looked down. "Maybe in the old days—we smoked a little pot, snorted some coke. Kid's stuff."

"How about out in California?"

"I don't know. I didn't know him out there."

"Who killed him, Bennie?"

He shook his head. "I don't know, man. I wish I did. The way they did him—that's some bad shit."

BACK at the *Ledger* offices I riffled through my notes and hashed together a piece on the Jaycees luncheon. I even recreated several quotations that spiced up Riley Hill's talk considerably. Eli Fullerton, the sportswriter, huffed and snorted at the desk beside me, pounding at his keyboard, chain-smoking. Leyland sat sequestered in his office.

Connie Perkins, the office gofer, passed by my desk and dropped off a copy of today's edition.

"Hot off the presses," she said, as she inevitably did every day about this time.

I grabbed the paper, and was amazed to find my story of the lynching had been buried on page three instead of the front page I felt it merited. Eli Fullerton glanced up as I mouthed half-audible oaths.

"What's up, Nelson?" he grunted, eyeing me from his desk.

I rapped today's edition against my leg emphatically. "I can't believe Leyland buried my story on page three."

He shook his head sorrowfully. "Hey. I'm sorry about that, buddy. Which story you talking about?"

Eli, of course, read little outside the sports pages and was oblivious to most of what went on in the world.

"The story on the lynching!" I said. "A black kid gets strung up like it's still 1950 and he buries it below an ad for Kmart."

He wrinkled his eyebrows. "Another black kid got strung up? Man, that's awful."

"What do you mean, 'another'?"

"Third one since this time last year," he said.

"Three? All lynched?"

He thought for a second. "No. One was drowned in the lake. Man, it's gonna start playing hell with out-of-state recruiting for football if this gets around."

"Three in the past year? What do the police say?"

He shrugged. "Beats me. Happened out in the county. Sheriff never came up with much."

"When was the last murder?"

"Last fall. Just after the Penn State game. That would've been in November."

Leyland came rumbling out of the office. "Afternoon deadline's coming up, Nelson," he drawled. "Better get that copy in."

"Leyland," I asked, "what about these two previous lynchings? Why didn't you tell me about these when I filed my story this morning?"

He stared me down coolly. "Didn't have anything to do with this one," he said.

"How do you know that?"

Again he let the air hang silent for a moment. I could hear the wind whistling in and out his nostrils and rattling in his emphysemic chest.

"Colored boys get themselves killed once in a while," he said. "They do crazy things—steal cars, get drunk, shoot each other up."

"Is that why you buried my story on page three?"

"I'd hardly call page three *buried*."

"This was a murder, Leyland, possibly racially motivated! How often do you get news like that in this little town?"

He shook his head. "This isn't Richmond or Cleveland, Nelson. Folks live in a town like Litchfield to get away from places like that. The last thing they want is to pick up their own little afternoon daily and see blood splattered across page one. We printed it; we just didn't hit people over the head with it."

I stood speechless for a moment.

"Now, file your stories so we can start blocking out tomorrow's edition," he said, and walked on toward the bathroom.

I was fuming but did not know quite how to answer Leyland.

I looked at my watch. It was almost two o'clock. Rayburn would be expecting me for our afternoon meeting—a ritual of his, dating back to my teens and begun again since my return.

I was anxious to see him for a change, as I wanted to hear his perspective on last night's events. I sat back down, quickly tacked an end onto my story about the Jaycees, filed it on the computer, forwarded a copy to Leyland's terminal, then signed off.

Before leaving, I stopped by Connie's desk.

"Hey, Nelson," she said as I approached. "How you doing?"

"Fine, Connie," I said. "Listen, Eli tells me that two other young black men have died under strange circumstances in the last year."

She thought for a moment. "Two. That's right."

"Could you pull the stories from the archive for me?"

"Sure, Nelson," she said.

I nodded and thanked her, then headed for the door before Leyland could return from the bathroom.

7

Wednesday Afternoon

UNCLE Rayburn waited at his usual bench on the edge of the town square, although his detached manner did not betray a hint of waiting on anything. He sat in his usual dress—stiffly starched white shirt, the long sleeves secured by gold cuff links, seersucker slacks, brightly polished oxfords. He watched my approach, his eyebrows wrinkled in furrows, nodding curtly as I sat.

His demeanor was disinterested, lordly, yet obliging, silver hair combed lankly back from a high forehead, cold blue eyes assaying the world through gold-rimmed bifocals. He was the last of us with any of the Old South in him. Two generations bereft of the land, one generation removed from any wealth, he nevertheless retained the carriage and manners of the landed gentry—unendingly polite, civil beyond all endurance, yet reticent to the point of being an enigma to all but his closest friends.

"Afternoon," I said as I took my place beside him.

The heat of the day was reaching its peak, the winds stilled, the air hanging warm and humid. Thunderheads trundled across the sky, but bore no signs of impending rain. The Courthouse Square lay green and quiet around us, disturbed only by the light traffic on this languorous Wednesday afternoon.

"How's business?" Rayburn asked finally, canting his head half in my direction.

"Fine," I said, not wanting to come immediately to my topic. "How's the hardware store?"

"Slow this time of year," he replied. "Folks have already done their spring planting and fix-up. Now the weather's turning warm, they lose the desire for yard work."

"It's a seasonal business," I said, savoring the emptiness of the comment.

"That it is," he replied, seeing no emptiness at all.

"Did you see my story in the newspaper?" I asked finally.

He paused for an instant before replying. "The one on the lynching?" he asked. "Yes, I saw it." His tone was noncommittal.

Silence hung between us.

"Nicely written," he said.

"Heard any talk around town about it?"

"Not much. You know how folks talk and never say anything."

"Who do you think's behind it?"

He paused again, considering. "Hard to say. Don't know much about the boy."

"What about the Klan? Doesn't it look like their work?"

Again he let silence hang in the air, as if he did not enjoy the conversation and felt I should wait for my answers.

Race relations, especially unpleasant ones, were not a topic folks of Rayburn's class enjoyed talking about. There was a certain *noblesse oblige* that the white gentry brought to matters of race—a subtext of unspoken privilege and obligation. When things went so badly and publicly wrong that a young black man ended up lynched, it implied that the obligations were not being respected and therefore the privilege might no longer be legitimate. It threatened to open Pandora's box and air all the grievances and bad blood of the last two hundred years. Things ran smoothly on the day-to-day in the South only by a collective denial of the history of the last two centuries, and by a scrupulous silence from our black brethren about the unpleasant facts of kidnapping, slavery, segregation, economic neglect, and oppression.

"The Klan?" Rayburn said distastefully. "Maybe twenty years ago, but not now. The Klan got pretty much broken up since they lost that civil suit in '79."

"What suit?" I asked, feigning ignorance, wanting to hear him tell it.

He turned and looked at me skeptically. "The suit your father brought way back in '58. After he died, it sat for a while then got expanded and refiled by some ACLU lawyers. Took the local Klan to civil court and skinned them for every nickel they had. They had to sell all their property and just drifted apart after that. You're lucky not many remember it was an Ingram that first got that going."

"What about Junior Cunningham?"

"Bubba Cunningham's boy? He just plays make-believe in his garage with a few other crazy white boys. They don't amount to half a minute of trouble."

"Maybe they're trying to change their image."

He sniffed. "Bubba never was worth a damn; I'd be surprised if Junior's any different."

"Who else would want to hang him? As far as I can tell, he was a model citizen."

He shrugged. "Long since gave up trying to figure people." *People* was slightly inflected, meaning black people. "If I were you, I'd stick to the plain facts of this and stop trying to play detective."

Neither of us spoke for several moments.

"How's Aunt Lucille doing?" I asked finally.

"Doing just fine," he said. "She's still wondering when you'll be coming over to supper."

"Soon. Tell her I'll come over soon."

"What about tonight?" he asked, turning to look at me.

I fidgeted under his gaze. "Sure. Tonight."

"Good. She'll be pleased."

He rose. "Got to get back to the store," he said.

I stood with him. "What time?" I asked.

He pulled out his gold railroad watch, flipped it open, and eyed the face. "Six o'clock," he said, nodded crisply at me, and strode off to the hardware store, his step still springy and brisk.

I rolled my eyes, dreading the prospect of an evening

with Lucille's fawning and gushing. Nevertheless, these obligations needed to be respected. I crossed the Courthouse Square and headed toward the police station.

Litchfield still appeared to be the epitome of the sleepy Southern town. The white-pillared Courthouse stood like a diminutive Roman temple at the head of the square. Across the square sat the squat, workmanlike Town Hall. In the center of the square stood the inevitable memorial for those lost in The War for Southern Independence—in Litchfield's case a marble statue of a Confederate foot soldier, his uniform tattered, but his carriage unvanquished, his gaze fixed on the horizon, aloof and proud.

The statue stood in the middle of a small patch of grass, around which were arranged stone benches where the town elders assembled themselves daily. When the weather was good, they generally held court there over the long lunch hour. For as long as I could remember, Rayburn had sat there through the middle part of the day, exchanging pleasantries with passersby, playing checkers, observing and codifying the day's events, the month's scandals. Indeed, for generations Ingram men had been gathering there. On the limited stage of Litchfield, their exploits made for occasionally distracting theater that was often the best you could get a thousand miles from Broadway.

Great-great-grandfather Benjamin Ingram moved to Litchfield in 1858 from Virginia. He was the third son of a plantation family and came down this way in the hopes of creating an agricultural fortune of his own in Alabama's fertile Black Belt. Staked by his father, he bought some acreage south of town, but before he could develop it, the war intervened. He left his wife to tend the land while he accepted a captain's post in the cavalry. Unfortunately, he lost his life to dysentery soon after the Battle of Vicksburg. Rather than take a respectable Union bullet, poor Ben died shitting his insides out in some Confederate hospital tent. It was, as it would turn out, an archetypally absurd Ingram death.

Just before leaving for war, Benjamin had managed to impregnate his wife, Elsie. She gave birth to a boy in the company of only a Negro midwife. She named him Op, after a beloved uncle and as a slap to her husband, who had left her pregnant and in charge of a plantation that was half gone to weeds with the other half swamp for at least a third of the year. Widowed by the middle of the war, she put the plantation in the hands of the foreman, told him to do what he could, and retired to the manse to nurse her grudges.

Op was raised mainly by the hired help and, as soon as he was of age, was sent off to boarding school. He returned after college and law school a dazed and abstracted man. He married a woman below his class, ran the plantation the rest of the way into the ground, sold off the land piecemeal, and moved into town to begin the now habitual Ingram path of eking out a living practicing law. He died uneventfully at an advanced age and bequeathed what was left of the Ingram land to his eldest son, Curry.

Curry Ingram, my grandfather, lost the balance of the Ingram fortune through bad business dealings and a naïve trust in the intentions of others. Whatever good investments he had went bad in the Crash of '29. He was left finally with only his Princeton law degree and an office off the Courthouse Square. Unfortunately, he also had the fatal Ingram attraction for lost causes. In his era, this led him to fight a series of losing labor actions and workman's compensation cases in a state where labor law became sketchy beyond protecting employees from indentured servitude. With his wife, Audrey, he produced my father and my Uncle Rayburn, as well as a third child lost to diphtheria. Late in life, depressed over the downward state of his affairs and his lack of financial security, he attempted suicide with a pistol.

Fortunately or not, he flinched at the last moment, succeeding in only blowing off his right ear and part of his cheek. Doc Compton, the now mythical town general practitioner, pulled him through the bleeding and infection and depressed funk. Over two months in the hospital, Curry healed up, dried out, wrestled with his demons, and decided to get on with things. On the day he was to return home, filled with a new desire to live, he dropped dead in the lobby of the hospital from a pulmonary embolus. Once again, the Fates had laughed at the Ingrams and laid them low with a sucker punch.

My father, Nelson, Sr., inherited Curry's tendency to depression, vainglorious do-gooding, and love of alcohol. My mother was a manic-depressive dipsomaniac from an old Birmingham family with plenty of social credentials but limited assets. They settled into an amiable alcoholic rut that allowed them both to get by. My father, like Curry before him, pursued the law, but managed to pick enough unpopular fights to keep his practice from taking off and to bar him from the inner circles of local power. I think he was well on his way to doing Curry one better and kill himself properly when the Ingram absurdity intervened.

MY afternoon rounds took me by the Litchfield police station to check the arrest log for the day. As always, Sergeant Beatty sat behind the front desk, his jaws working a chaw of tobacco. He eyed my approach coolly.

"Ain't nothing happened today, Ingram," he said.

I edged up to his desk and glanced through the arrest log—nothing of significance recorded since yesterday.

"Any news on the lynching?" I asked.

"That's county business," he answered brusquely.

"I thought the city provided liaison assistance with detective work."

"The county ain't asked for no assistance far as I know."

I raised my eyebrows. "Really?"

"Really," he replied sarcastically.

OUTSIDE the police station the sky was darkening as the sun fell behind the storm clouds. Officers Sonny Trottman and Billy Majors were standing at the curb, about to climb into their patrol car for the evening shift. I nodded in their general direction.

"Nelson!" Sonny called. Sonny and I had gone to high school together. Although we had never been friends, ever since my return to Litchfield he had treated me like some long-lost fraternity brother.

"Hey, Sonny." I ambled over.

"How you doing, buddy?" he asked warmly.

He laid a beefy hand across my back and smiled, giving me the full flash of his mirrored aviator sunglasses. His teeth glistened. His breath wafted toward me, a mixture of stale coffee, cigarettes, and this evening's barbecue. Sonny had been a tackle for the high school team and had even served briefly as third string on one of Bear Bryant's teams in the late sixties before poor grades and lack of stand-out ability forced him out of college and into police work. He was a tall, squarely built slab of a man, gone more to fat as he pushed forty, but nevertheless an intimidating piece of flesh. He had been on the Litchfield police for twenty years and was prince of the evening shift. He might have risen higher had he not had a penchant for the occasional lost weekend that turned into a lost week spent drinking and carousing in Louisiana or Florida.

"I'm doing just fine, Sonny," I said.

"Good," he said, smiling broadly again. "Gettin' settled in?"

"Oh, yeah. Getting settled in just fine."

"Bet that old fish camp needs a little work after all these years," he said.

"It's a bit run down," I said, "but it's quiet out there."

"I remember when I was a kid I used to sneak out there and drop a pole off your father's dock. Used to be some good catfish off that bank." Sonny smiled as he said this, tilting up his sunglasses and looking fondly into the distance.

"Still are good catfish up that part of the river," his partner, Billy Majors, chimed in. He was a beanpole of a boy, blond and fair-cheeked with a pinched face. His uniform was crisply starched and a size too large; he looked all of sixteen standing there, pulling at his gun belt and smiling obligingly. "Caught a slew of 'em up near your daddy's place just last month."

"The dock's washed away," I said, "but you're welcome to drop by anytime and toss in a line from the bank."

"I just might do that some weekend," Sonny said.

"Heard anything 'bout that lynching last night?"

"Nothing much. County's been mighty tight-lipped."

"Listen, Sonny," I said, hoping that this might be a ripe moment to steer personal reveries into matters of business. "As slow as news is around here, I don't want to miss any good stories. I'd surely appreciate it if y'all could give me a call at home if you get wind of any action on evening shifts. If I hadn't had my police scanner on last night, I would've missed that lynching story." I pulled out my notepad, wrote my phone number down, and gave it to him.

He held the slip of paper for an instant. I could feel him weighing the issue, trying to decide if there was something wrong with this. Unsure, he dropped his sunglasses back over his eyes and stuck the paper in his shirt pocket.

"Sure, Nelson," he said without enthusiasm. "No problem."

"You can count on us, Nelson," Billy said, smiling broadly.

"Get in the car, Billy," Sonny said, irritated. Billy fumbled in his pocket for the keys to the patrol car.

Sonny leaned close to me. "You got a gun out there at your daddy's place?" he said half under his breath.

I stared at him blankly. "I've got my father's old shotgun."

He pulled me close and put his face up to mine. I got the full aroma of his breath again.

"You need to keep it handy," he said. "There's been some things going on out there north of the lake."

"Things?"

"I can't tell you the half of it." He looked around as if checking to see if anyone was listening. Billy leaned out the window of the patrol car, looking eagerly at the two of us talking.

"Goddamnit!" Sonny said to him. "Don't just sit there drawing flies. Roll up the windows, start the engine, and get the AC running!"

Billy complied sheepishly. The patrol car's engine thrummed into life and the windows slid up.

"Listen, Nelson," Sonny said, "there's some shit goin' down out there in the county. I only heard rumors but they're all bad. You need to keep your head down, keep your doors locked, and stay clear of trouble."

"Shit, Sonny. You gotta tell me more than that!"

"Cain't tell you no more," he said. He tipped his glasses up again and regarded me seriously. "But you call me if you get wind of anything."

"But that's out in the county, outside police jurisdiction."

"Just call me and let me worry about that."

I nodded. "You call me, too, Sonny. I don't want to miss a story."

He punched me affectionately on the shoulder and climbed into the passenger side of the patrol car. He waved once as Billy squealed the tires dramatically and pulled out into the street.

BACK at the office, I found on my desk copies of the news stories on the two murders from the last year that Eli had mentioned. Connie had left them for me before she went home.

The first one was a year ago in July—a twenty-two-year-old named Isaiah Jackson found lynched near Banfield. The next was a twenty-eight-year-old named James Davidson found drowned in the Sour Mash River about a mile downstream from my father's fish camp last November. Both articles were the barest of stories—nothing beyond a bald statement of the facts. I scribbled the names and the pertinent details in my notebook. Tomorrow I would have to see if the police had any more details.

The newsroom was quiet. The day had passed in a blur. I now faced dinner with Rayburn and Lucille—an adventure that took a certain poise and frame of mind, even on the best of days. I rubbed my eyes, feeling suddenly tired. I was in desperate need of a drink.

I looked at my watch. Four forty-five.

I had made a pledge when I got this job that I would not drink until after five on working days, but I figured by the time I got to the Crimson 'n' White, the deadline would have passed.

8

Wednesday Evening

THE Crimson 'n' White was a quiet bar a couple of blocks off the town square. The walls were checkered with dusty Alabama football memorabilia and Bear Bryant portraits depicting the various epiphanies in the life of the legendary coach: The Bear and Namath hunched together on the sideline in an oil painting entitled, "Third and Long"; The Bear on the sidelines, porkpie hat cocked confidently forward, one hand thrust ahead, wielding a rolled-up copy of a game plan like a baton, entitled, "The Bear and 315," immortalizing his record-breaking 315th victory as coach. Another charcoal portrait hung above the bar, autographed in a broad hand by the Coach himself.

The Bear was five years dead, yet his ghost still rattled around Alabama, as haunting as the Civil War dead, as annoying as Elvis's unburiable specter. I think the origin of his overpowering presence lay back in the 1960's. He preached hard work and honor and guts. He drank and smoked and cursed, and any Alabama man could see that The Bear was not too far removed from himself. While George Wallace was standing in the schoolhouse door and freedom riders were being beaten and Bull Conner was turning fire hoses and dogs on black children, The Bear had gone quietly about the business of winning football games and national championships, giving Alabama bragging rights at least in this one arena when so much else here was shameful or shabby or backward.

I made my way to the bar and ordered a beer. Jerome, the bartender, acknowledged me with a cursory grunt. Although I had come here after work every day for the last three weeks, I had yet to attain the status of a regular and so had to spell all requests out. Nothing yet was assumed. That is one of the great charms of the South—for all their *y'all-come* hospitality, they were as wary of strangers and newcomers as the British.

Jerome was a big sullen man, long bored with the superficial niceties of bartending and settled into a tolerant but disinterested rut. He would rouse himself to discuss the daily news with the regulars, occasionally achieving transient animation when the subjects of football or duck hunting made their appearance, but for the stranger off the street, the greeting was terse.

I had found this place by accident, but it was my Platonic Form of The Bar—anonymity preserved, nothing asked, little expected. Beer and quiet—the high point of any evening when one of the pensioners chose to amble to the jukebox and crank up Mel Tillis or Hank Williams. After a year or two of time served I might be elected quietly to "Regular" status and be no longer required to order my drinks in detail, but it would be a subtle and unheralded thing, passed over with barely an acknowledgment.

Jerome had the good taste to subscribe to the local paper, as well as the Birmingham and Atlanta dailies. I could spend these late afternoons browsing the newsprint while I sipped Budweiser. The great heap of felonies and murders that burdened a single news day in Atlanta made my own little murder seem rather quaint. Except that now it appeared that I might have three murders to explain. Three murders, no motives, and only a pair of questionable suspects. Where to go next? Clearly, I had to dig deeper into the histories of the other two victims and see if there were any connections.

I sighed at the thought of the work that this involved and wondered why I was bothering at all. Leyland certainly didn't care about the story and would just as soon see it buried in a single paragraph on page ten. Pursuing it was likely only to antagonize him, and nosing around the community asking questions about lynchings and hate crimes was not going to win me any friends either. Still, my instincts told me that there was a story here and maybe a big one. In the back of my mind I couldn't help but think that maybe it would be a big enough story to get my name back out there and maybe land me a real job outside this godforsaken county. On the other hand, maybe it would be just enough of a story to alienate my boss and lose me this job.

I idled my way through the beer and shuffled

through the newspapers. The bar began to fill up with the happy hour crowd. I ordered a second beer and moved off toward a quieter corner. An old-timer with unusual taste had wandered up to the jukebox and punched up Sinatra singing "The Summer Wind." It was one of those rare splendid moments—the fine bite of the beer, the crowd's hectic backdrop, and Sinatra.

A blonde came in and made her way to the bar. She hoisted herself onto a barstool and pulled out a cigarette. I stared at her and tried to decide. It was Connie from work.

She placed an order and Jerome produced the drink. He exchanged a few words with her and she smiled and then looked away, staring off into the middle distance, sipping at the whiskey absently. She scanned the room and then saw me. She waved coyly and smiled.

It had been a long time since I'd seen a woman direct such a look toward me. I knew enough to be extremely wary of them from any woman, let alone from a woman with whom I worked. I nodded in reply to her wave and then pretended absorption in the *Birmingham News*.

Out of the corner of my eye, I saw her leave the barstool.

"Hey, Nelson," she said, closing in. "You a regular here?"

I looked up, cornered. "Only been in town a few weeks. Hard to be a regular anywhere," I said, shrugging.

She slid into the booth across the table from me. "I thought you grew up in Litchfield," she said.

"Been gone for a while."

"I heard," she said, pulling at her cigarette. "So where you been?"

I'd really not paid much attention to her at the office. She was our pool secretary and general gofer. She looked to be on the high side of twenty-five, but well short of forty.

I laughed. "That's a long story."

"I got time," she said.

I shook my head. "Really, it's just a long, bad country song."

"Don't give me that," she said, patting me remonstratively on the back of my hand. "You're a famous reporter. I've seen your clippings." Where she'd touched me burned like fire. I couldn't remember how long it had been since I'd been touched by a woman.

"Where'd you see my clippings?" I asked.

"Leyland's got them in his office. He shows them to folks when you're not around."

"What? To gloat that he's got my ass working for him down in Litchfield?"

"He's proud, silly," she said, patting me on the hand again. "He'd kill me if he knew I was telling you."

I found myself blushing and quickly changed the topic. "So what about you?" I asked. "How long have you been with the paper?"

She snorted. "Forever. It's like I came with the office furniture."

I tried to change the subject, commenting how Litchfield had changed since I'd been back last.

"Yeah," she said. "The Feds closed the paper mill and all the jobs left town. They built the mall out along the Interstate and all the downtown stores closed up.

And they built a dog track that brings in riffraff from three states."

"Well, at least the track brings in jobs and money."

"Six full-time jobs they gave to people from out of town, and the rest is seasonal work. And all the money goes to the state racing commission or into the county treasury and's never heard from again."

I shrugged.

"What you writing?" she asked, looking at my open notebook.

"Just trying to put something together on that lynching last night."

"Just some kid got himself strung up," she said matter-of-factly.

"That seems to be more or less what everyone has heard," I said. "You'd think lynchings were like car accidents around here—they just kinda happen."

"I don't know," she said. "I got enough to worry about."

I was beginning to get a little irritated with the indifference I ran into everywhere.

"What is it about this place?" I asked rhetorically. "This isn't Detroit or L.A. Why doesn't anyone seem to give a damn about this?"

Connie took a final drag from her cigarette then stubbed it out.

"Honey," she said, "this town is down on its luck and tired of hearing about it. Ever since the paper mill and the Goodyear plant closed, folks ain't had a minute of good times and they ain't up to your idea of what they should act like."

I smiled. "Sorry. Don't mean to preach."

She shook her head. "Just listen to me. You'd think I gave a hoot about any of that." She leaned in and took my hand again. "But if I was you, honey, I'd lighten up on this lynching. It's gonna be either a dead end or a world of trouble."

"To get along, you got to go along. Is that it?" I drawled, smiling thinly.

"Now you're talking." She looked at me and smiled. "Now, I came here to have a good time. What are you doing tonight?"

I coughed. "I'm afraid I've got a dinner engagement already."

Her face dropped noticeably.

I smiled. "I'm having supper with my aunt and uncle. How about a drink afterward. About eight-thirty or nine?"

She brightened at the banality of my evening plans.

"Maybe," she said, taking out a notepad and scribbling something on the front page. "Call me when you're finished."

She pulled back and tried to seem distant. "Maybe I'll still be free for the evening."

I smiled and graciously accepted the slip of paper.

9

Wednesday Evening

UNCLE Rayburn and I sat out on the front porch after dinner, sipping toddies and watching the evening approach. The meal had been a familiar affair—the table laden with Lucille's silver and Wedgwood, the chicken and greens and okra steaming in their serving trays, Lucille hovering and twittering like an ancient nervous bird. She had changed not a bit—effusive, overbearing, prying, with a barrage of questions, mixed with an endless flow of local news and updates on great-aunts and cousins thrice-removed who were little more than blurs in my memory. Rayburn, as was his wont, sat silent as his wife carried the weight of the dinner's conversation, occasionally offering a nod or a half-swallowed word. Only after the meal did he assert himself and invite me out to the porch to sit with him while Lucille looked after the kitchen.

Dusk gathered around us as we sat in the porch rockers. Cicadas thrummed quietly in the bushes and Lucille clattered in the kitchen. A thin breeze drifted across the porch.

"Sort of evening your father liked," Rayburn said.

"Daddy liked anything that involved drinking," I said.

Rayburn inclined his head in my direction and cut his eyes toward me.

"Your father drank," he said. "No one denies that. He drank more than his share, but he carried more than his share. You should know that. I'm surprised you don't remember more about him."

"I'm sorry," I said. "I remember plenty about him."

Silence fell between us again, only the creak of the porch rockers in the air.

"Seems to me that you remember what you want to about him," he said.

"I remember him plenty well," I replied.

"He was my brother," Rayburn said. "I knew him. He was a complicated man. He had standards that he couldn't live up to."

Rayburn paused for a moment, then went on.

"He made mistakes, his will failed him at times, but he lived by his lights and he had spine. More'n you can say about most."

He rocked back and forth more vigorously. He had said his piece—for Rayburn it could pass for a day's worth of talking.

We sat together in silence for a long while. The floorboards creaked under the rails of the rockers.

Lucille bustled out onto the porch and summoned us in for dessert.

AFTER my father died, my mother collapsed into a stupor of grief and alcohol, from which, despite generous tinctures of time and sympathy, she never emerged. Rayburn and Aunt Lucille took my mother and me into their house when it became clear that we could not manage on our own. They were a childless couple already well into middle age, set in their ways. Their Victorian house on a tidy half-acre just outside of town was a dark and cluttered place, full of things delicate and sentimental—little porcelain mementos, china tea services, and leaded crystal. It was not a place intended for a child. A teenager in any form is an embarrassment to God's handiwork, tolerated only because of ontogeny's relentless demands; one as recalcitrant and sullen as myself had to have been a saintly burden for them.

My mother proved an even greater burden. For two years she was an erratic drunken missile in the house, useless and disruptive, alternately tearful and tyrannical, drunk for days at a stretch, coming to supper in her nightgown, disheveled and reeking of whiskey. Rayburn locked up his liquor. She sent out for it by taxi, switching to gin so he couldn't smell it on her breath. Rayburn called the cab company and stopped the errands. She suddenly became able again to go out on her own.

When I was fifteen, she made her first suicide attempt—a wrist-slashing gesture that spattered the bathroom sink and walls. Rayburn put her away quietly in the state hospital. Within a year she was out again, set up in a small apartment nearby. I stayed with Rayburn and Lucille and she was brought over to visit once a month for Sunday dinner. She was usually so deep into one of her black funks that there was little beyond perfunctory exchanges. She had never been the warmest of mothers, and now she was only an empty reminder of a childhood I never really had. At eighteen I went off to college, gladly leaving her and Litchfield behind.

Two years ago at Christmastime, she telephoned. We had not spoken in more than a decade. I had just been fired from a job with a paper in Florida and was sitting sullenly in my apartment drinking.

"Hello, Nelson," she said, the voice half lost in the static of the line, "it's Marian. Your mother."

From the gentle slur in her Southern drawl I surmised that she had been drinking as well. "Marian," I thought to myself, the strangeness of the name ringing in my ears.

"Mother!" I said, surprised and pleased, yet baffled again as to what to say. "Good to hear from you."

"I got your number from Rayburn," she said. "I thought I'd call to wish you Merry Christmas. . . ." Her voice trailed off.

"How're you doing?"

"Fine," she said. "And you? How's work?"

"Fine," I lied. "Work's going great. . . ."

The conversation staggered on. I imagined that I was able to cover my state, but in truth it was a sad exchange. Later I reflected on how our plights had come together—two maudlin drunks trying to communicate over hundreds of miles and twenty years.

When Rayburn called me in Key West and told me that she had died, I felt little, drunk again. When I pulled myself together, I scraped up bus fare and my few belongings. Over a day and a half on a Greyhound I cleared the sludge of my hangover and slowly began to make my first pass at understanding.

My parents were gone. Although I had gone for decades with scarcely an acknowledgment of my mother, I always knew she was there. With her gone, I felt more alone than I had ever been. At two in the morning in a brightly lit bus stop in Dothan, Alabama, staring into a cup of black coffee, tears stung my eyes and I felt something rip in my chest. I boarded the bus again, dazed and drained. The dawn stirred over the green Alabama fields.

Rayburn met me at the bus station in Litchfield at midday. He looked me up and down, noting my tattered jacket and ragged jeans, but saying little. His cryptic visage had not changed. He drove me to his house, and we spoke his terse code language.

At the funeral, there was a huge gathering—a din of voices and crush of bodies. Even though she had been an outcast for nearly three decades, her death had drawn the community together. Families that had not spoken since I was a child came under the same roof and were civil to each other, if not amicable.

In her open casket, my mother appeared waxy and quite dead. I stood beside her in the dim parlor. Rayburn came up next to me. We stood together in silence for a long moment.

"Pour me a drink, Rayburn," I said.

"A little early," he said.

"Today's special."

He nodded. We moved quietly into the back room of the funeral parlor. He pulled a pair of Dixie cups from beside the water cooler and a hip flask suddenly appeared in his hand as if by magic. He poured a generous shot into each cup, capped the flask, and quickly slid it back into an inside pocket of his coat. We sipped at the sour mash and rocked back and forth on our heels. The leather of my new shoes creaked.

"Nelson," he said finally, "what the hell are you doing with yourself?"

I took a healthy slug of whiskey. "I don't know."

"How old are you? Thirty-six, thirty-seven?"

"Thirty-nine."

"Thirty-nine years old and out of work without two dimes to rub together."

"That's right," I said. The whiskey bit at me, hot and smoky.

"The editor of the paper here is a friend of mine. I might could get you work."

"Rayburn, I appreciate the offer, but I think I'll be able to line something up myself. I'll handle things."

He snorted. "Boy, you don't even have money for bus fair! How're you going to line anything up? You owe me two hundred dollars for that suit you're wearing—how're you gonna pay that back? Tell me, boy, I'm interested how you're gonna *handle things*? You're thirty-nine years old and you couldn't handle a frying pan if I gave you a hot pad!"

I took another big slug of whiskey and swished it around in my mouth, unable to answer him.

"Let me tell you," Rayburn went on, his voice softening, "when your daddy passed, it was no secret that your mother wasn't up to looking after you. So I became responsible for you. But now I feel like I let your daddy down. Your life's a mess, son. You need help. I want you to let me give it to you."

I could find little to say. I looked up at him and found his steely blue eyes staring hard at me.

He was right. What was I to do? I nodded at him and bowed my head.

"Thank you, Uncle," I said quietly.

10

Wednesday Evening

I HAD called Connie Perkins just before leaving Rayburn's house and asked her out for a drink. After following her complicated directions, getting lost twice, I pulled up to the curb opposite a low-set white frame house lit only by a yellow porch light. I didn't even know why I was doing it. I guessed I had spent a few too many nights now holed up out at the river cabin alone.

I leaned my head out the car window and drew in a deep breath. The air was warm and heavy, scented with legustrum. I climbed out, feeling far too old to be dating anyone, let alone someone who must have been ten years younger than me.

The door opened promptly at my knock and Connie stood backlit in the entry hall.

"Let's go, sugar," she said. "Time's a wasting."

She stepped out onto the porch and locked the door behind her. She had her hair up and wore a tightly fitting dress cut above the knee.

"Oh, Lord," she said, inclining her head toward the curb, "is that your car?"

"Uh—yes," I said.

"Guess I should've dressed down a little more."

"Sorry."

"Don't make no different," she said, taking me by the arm.

I opened the door for her and she settled herself daintily into the seat. I climbed behind the wheel.

"Where're we going?" she asked, checking her makeup in the passenger side mirror.

"I hadn't thought much about it," I said, starting the car.

"Glad to see you've put so much into this," she said sarcastically, reaching out and tugging at my tie. "All dressed up, too."

"Give me a break. I haven't been out on a date in years."

"All right, honey."

"Where d'you want to go?"

She primped at her hair. "Well, let me see. . . ."

I pulled away from the curb slowly. "If you don't decide soon, we're going to end up back at the Crimson 'n' White."

"Oh, shoot no!"

"Well, then, where?"

"Get on 69 going north. I know a little place out by

the lake." She flipped on the radio and tuned it to a country-and-western station.

I turned onto Highway 69 and headed north.

We drove without speaking for quite a while.

"So, where are we going?" I asked finally.

"A little place out by the lake—The Watering Hole."

"Never heard of it."

"A few things have changed in the time you've been away," she said sarcastically.

THE Watering Hole sat at the end of a little access road off State Road 227, the parking lot illuminated by a single floodlight, the building distinguished by only a red neon sign in the window proclaiming the bar's name. We pulled onto the parking lot. Connie was halfway out of the car before I had come to a stop.

"C'mon," she said. "Time's wasting."

"Trying to get in ahead of me so you can pretend you're here alone?"

She turned to look at me over her shoulder, cracking a smile. "Course not. I just want to make you work a little."

The bar was dimly lit and smoky. We sifted through a maze of tables populated by shadowed faces and clouds of tobacco smoke. I followed Connie toward the far corner of the room where a table sat empty. She slid into the chair against the wall and kicked a chair clear from the table for me.

It was a large open room, lit only by the sputtering glow of candles on the tables and a few lights at the bar opposite the door. Considering it was a weekday, the crowd was respectable. In the half-light I could not easily make out many faces, but they seemed to be a tonier set than one might expect from a roadside joint out in the country. Quite a few suits and ties shared tables with ladies in dresses. A waitress sifted between the tables and leaned over for our order. Connie seized the moment and ordered us two beers.

"So tell me," she said, leaning in toward me, "how many wives did you leave behind out there in the world?" She smiled wryly.

"Just one. A few girlfriends. No children I'm aware of."

The waitress sifted through the crowd and brought our beer.

"What was she like? The wife," Connie asked.

I took a long pull at my beer.

"She was . . . remarkable. Rich, pretty, smart. Everything a man could want." I stared off into space.

"So what happened?"

"What happened? I fucked it up. I was no good for her. She had that brought home to her one too many times, so she divorced me."

A plump balding fellow in a tartan sports coat emerged from the gloom off to my right and leaned over our table.

"Connie!" he said in a soft Southern drawl. "Long time."

He pulled out a chair and sat down, a haze of musk and aftershave coming off him.

"Tommy!" Connie cried. "I want you to meet a friend of mine. This is Nelson Ingram." She grabbed my shoulder and gave it a squeeze. "Nelson, this is Tommy Sheehy—he owns the place."

"Pleased to meet you," Sheehy said, offering a handshake.

I nodded and smiled.

"Actually, I'm just the manager," he went on. "She's just callin' me the owner to flatter some free drinks out of me."

"Oh, Tommy, really!"

He smiled at Connie and pulled out a cigar. "You new in town, Mr. Ingram?" he asked.

His face was round and double-chinned. One would think him almost avuncular if it were not for his eyes, which were quick and hard. They missed nothing.

I nodded again. "I'm with the *Ledger*."

"Really." His tone was polite but he became several degrees more removed, leaning back in his chair and assaying me.

"He's all right, Tommy," Connie said.

"That a fact?"

"He grew up right here in Litchfield!" she said. "He's just been away for a while."

He nodded and twirled his fingers in his lap.

"You from around here?" I asked him.

He caught me in his gaze, holding his eyes there a moment, then answered deliberately. "That's right. I went up North to work for a while. Came back a few years ago."

"And he's worked wonders with this tired old bar," Connie said, waxing effusive.

Sheehy barely waved an index finger at a waitress

and two more beers appeared for us, as well as a bourbon for him.

"So, Mr. Ingram, where you been all the years you were away?"

"I might ask you the same question."

"I asked first."

"Here and there," I said.

"Me, too," Sheehy said, his eyes glinting at me.

This was no ordinary saloonkeeper. Beneath his fat, moist exterior lay something flintier, something I had seen before but could not seem to place.

Connie leaned across the table. "Can I tell him, Tommy?" she hissed in mock confidentiality.

He looked at her then back at me.

"Tell him what you want," he said. His eyes stayed fixed on her, though, and she did not say any more.

After a moment of awkward silence, a waiter bent over and whispered in his ear. He nodded and rose.

"I have to be going," he said. "Nice meetin' you, Mr. Ingram."

He smiled, inclined his head in Connie's direction, and left us.

Connie leaned into me. "Tommy's had such an interesting past. I'm sure you two would just have so much to talk about."

"Sounds like you've spent a few nights here talking with him. What's so interesting about his past?"

She leaned closer into me. I felt her shoulder nuzzling under the crook of my arm, the soft swell of her breast against my chest.

"Tommy spent a few years up North, working for some of the *families* up there."

"Families?"

"You know. Those *Italian* families."

That was where I had seen it before. Tommy Sheehy was a soldier for a Mafia family. In Cleveland I had run across his type from time to time and had always been struck by their simultaneous banality and lethality. I would come upon them on odd evenings doing after-hours background work in the shadier parts of town. Knowing what I did of these sorts of people in those parts of Cleveland, I asked few questions, kept quiet, and never used my real name. In Richmond, I saw much less of their type, although organized crime had its role there, too—cocaine and heroin and gambling. Occasionally, one would run across them, sifting through a bar at night with the dull malevolence of sharks.

I sipped cautiously at my beer, wishing Connie had been more discrete in her introductions.

"So what's he doing here in Litchfield?" I asked finally.

She smiled sarcastically. "You know what they say, Nelson—you can take the boy out of the country but you can't take the country out of the boy."

"Right. He left New York out of lonesomeness for dear old 'Bama's nightlife."

"Well, he never confided in me. It's not like I know him that well."

I watched him now from a distance, perched at the corner of the bar, sipping at a drink, eyeing the room in a calculating manner. It made no sense for a man like him to be down here in this backwater.

I motioned to the waitress for two more beers. Conversation meandered, Connie leaning into me a little more with each round. I pulled myself away from her once to go to the bathroom. She had been in the middle of a detailed recounting of her divorce, but nature issued a call I could not ignore.

The air seemed murky as I picked my way between the tables. Sheehy sat at one end of the bar and followed me with his eyes. A man sat beside him, his back facing me. He appeared to be talking to Sheehy, gesturing emphatically but his voice subdued.

In the men's room, standing at ease before a urinal, I placed Tom Sheehy. I smelled the scent of urine mixed with Lysol and tobacco, and the memory came back to me—twenty years ago and more, there he had been, standing in a corner of the boys' room in school, a stocky older kid with greased-back hair, bad skin, and nervous eyes, smoking and watching the door. He wore straight-legged denims and a white cotton T-shirt like a uniform, eyeing the world in that same hard and malevolent fashion.

On my way back to my table I took another look at Sheehy, now seeing in him the young tough sagging and gone to fat, and took perverse delight that the years had not been unkind only to myself. Then I noticed that the person who still sat opposite him at the bar was a black man. This was of only minor interest until I recognized him as Malcolm, the brother-in-law of Reginald Copley.

I stopped at the bar and ordered two more beers from the bartender. Sheehy sat impassively as Malcolm leaned into him and gestured forcefully but compactly. Sheehy inclined his head in a half-nod, as if examining his shoes, and Malcolm leaned lower, trying to make eye contact. The bartender brought my order and I headed toward my table. Now Sheehy was looking up at Malcolm and speaking tight-lipped and evenly.

Connie smiled at my approach. "This place is getting old, Nelson honey," she said. "Why don't we head on?"

"You gotta finish your beer first," I said. "Otherwise, how can I get you drunk and take advantage of you?"

She mustered a coquettish smile. I turned to look back at the bar. Sheehy sat alone now and Malcolm was nowhere to be seen.

11

Thursday Morning

CONNIE and I hit a couple of other spots. She told me her stories; I doled out a few of mine. We had nothing in common, but it was still nice to spend time with someone other than my aunt and uncle. Finally, way past midnight I dropped her off at her house.

"Oh, I had a wonderful time," she drawled, in caricature as we stood at her front door.

"My pleasure," I said.

She hesitated, then leaned forward and pecked me primly on the cheek. "I'd invite you in, but you know, there's work tomorrow and . . ."

"No problem," I said, turning away from the abyss. "Gotta be up at the crack of dawn myself."

She opened the door and stepped inside. "You drive

careful now," she said, shutting the door slowly, smiling awkwardly.

I nodded and kept the smile pinned to my face as the door closed.

My smile had turned rueful as I headed back to the car. Dating in the post-AIDS era was a different beast entirely from what I remembered from the seventies. No sex, no drugs, no rock 'n' roll, both innocence and sentimentality gone, replaced by a sad and wary distance. I turned on the radio and tuned to the oldies station out of Birmingham. Neil Young's "The Needle and the Damage Done" came on. I turned up the volume and drove home.

I PULLED down the drive to my father's cabin and parked beside the steps. In these dead hours past midnight the woods still hummed and chattered. A single cicada raised the pitch of its frenetic song, then grew louder and louder still.

There are days in late summer or early autumn when cicadas seem to dominate the world. Walking through a freshly mown field in September or early October I would hear them, filling the field with their trilling. I remember it as a plaintive sound at summer's end; the weather hot, the trees thick with deep green leaves, but already there is a poignant slant to the noon sun. Behind the heat is a new fragility. Not the blasting heat of July—it has no presence, as if the slightest change in the wind could abolish it. Autumn is coming; the cicadas' day is ending, and so they sing loudly against its arrival.

I got out of the car and a twig crackled underfoot. I stopped. The sounds of the woods seemed to fall away and for a moment all was quiet and I had a sudden and unwanted memory of that day. It had been just a few hundred yards away along the bottomland downriver that he had died.

That day had been a warm, close October day. We had been at the river since early morning. Uncle Rayburn was there, along with my father's cousin from downstate. My father had been drinking heavily all day. Despite Rayburn's better judgment, my father had insisted on an afternoon shoot.

The sunlight slanted through the trees as the day lengthened, and despite the heat of the day, one had a foretaste of autumn in the air. To the north dark clouds huddled up. A warm wind came from the south, electricity in the air. My father's cousin set off ahead with his dogs and Rayburn walked off to his right. My father and I followed to the left. I walked behind my father. I remember the heaviness of his gait. The heat and the whiskey had gotten to him, and he was logy and inattentive. They flushed a covey, and my father fumbled with his gun halfheartedly. His cousin got a single as the covey scattered. The shotgun's flat reports filled the air, followed by the smell of gunpowder. My father cursed and reached for his hip flask.

The clouds reached up and covered the sun. One moment he was in light, the next swallowed up in the shadows. The wind died all at once. He swayed as he cocked his head back and took a short drink. He pivoted to turn toward me, branches crackling underfoot. His toe must have caught on something. He stumbled and fell forward.

I TRUDGED up the stairs to my little cabin, my only remaining inheritance from my father, trudging home like he had on any one of a thousand nights—drunk, dispirited, and in the grip of his *déjà vu*. I stripped off my shirt and pants and fell into bed.

I lay there for an hour, my mind whirring in a muddle. I remember that fall as if it had lasted years, singed into memory, coddled and fleshed out from endless recollection. His shotgun was riding loose on his hip, safety off. As he fell, it dropped from his grip. He flung his arms forward to catch himself. The gun spun as it fell, landing stock first on the ground. He fell toward it, the muzzle centered on his chest. I remember no noise, just the flash from the barrel followed by a lazy brown breath of smoke. He let out a grunt and settled heavily, slowly to the ground. The gun smoke swirled around us. The world seemed immobile. He coughed once, bringing up a gout of blood, then settled even more heavily into the ground. A red stain spread out around him in the red-orange fallen leaves.

I was on the edge of sleep when the phone rang. Full awake in a second, I rolled out of bed and stumbled into the living room, trying to remember where I had left the phone.

I finally found it on the floor beside a table.

"Hello?" I said.

"Nelson? That you?"

I could not place the voice at first, then I recognized it as Sonny Trottman's.

"Yeah," I said. "Hey, Sonny."

"Remember how you said to give you a call if we got wind of any action?" He sounded tense and tentative, not entirely comfortable with what he was doing.

"Yeah, Sonny." I sat down and rubbed my eyes. "What's up?"

"They got them another murder out in the county."

"Really? Where?" I reached for pen and paper.

"Up on 72, past the Williston turnoff."

"If it's out in the county, how did you get wind of it?"

"From the radio chatter. You can tell they're uptight. Two stiffs in two days is more than a deputy sheriff can tolerate."

I cursed my inattentiveness. I'd had my police scanner turned off because of the date with Connie.

"Listen, Sonny, thanks. I'll go check this out now. The murder scene's near the highway?"

"Yeah. Just off the shoulder, 'bout a quarter mile past the turnoff."

"Thanks, Sonny. Listen, you can come fish off my daddy's bank anytime."

"Thanks, Nelson. Gotta go. Bobby says we just got a call—Charlie Ray's beatin' up his old lady again. Shheeit! Why can't they drop these bodies inside city limits and give me something interesting to do!" He hung up.

THE murder site was a grassy patch off the shoulder of Highway 72 illuminated by blue-red strobes and headlights from a cordon of sheriff's cars. I pulled in short of the scene and walked quietly forward. Everyone was absorbed in their work and I was able to walk right up to the circle of officers that stood around the body. Cicadas thrummed in the still night, toads grumbled and croaked off in the bush, and the deputies stood and glumly contemplated the body where it lay, facedown in a narrow culvert just off the road.

"Well, Ingram," a voice said at my shoulder, "we just can't keep you away."

I turned. It was Sheriff Stanton on the job again in the dead of night. Did this man ever sleep?

I nodded. "A job's a job," I said.

He looked me up and down coolly.

"So what do you have, Sheriff?" I asked.

"Somebody saw a car slow and dump something big out on the side of the road. They came to check it out and found that." He nodded toward the body.

"Any ID?" I asked.

"Wallet says it's Thomas Sheehy. He runs a bar out near the lake."

"Really?" I said, pretending ignorance.

"Looks like he was shot several times in the chest and beaten." Stanton seemed considerably more agitated than he had been last night.

I stepped toward the body but Stanton cut me off. "Now, Ingram, you tried to fuck up the scene last night. Just leave this one to us."

I opened my mouth to protest, but he already had me by the arm and escorted me back toward my car.

"We'll have the full details in the morning," he said.

I craned my head to peer at the scene. Stanton opened my car door for me.

"But I've got a right to this story," I said.

He leaned close to me. "Son," he said quietly, "don't give me that 'freedom of the press' shit. This is my county. Don't make me throw your ass in jail."

"You can't do that."

He raised his eyebrows and laughed. "Try me."

I got into my car and he closed the door for me. He bent down and got in my face again through the open window. "Now that's the first smart thing I've seen you do in the last two days."

I smiled thinly and started the car. He rapped my hood affirmatively and turned back to the crime scene. I sat there a moment watching him walk away. The sky in the east was beginning to brighten at the approach of day.

I drove back to the cabin and showered, trying to force some energy into my flagging body. The treatment failed and I dressed wearily, dreading the day that lay ahead. Instant coffee made with warm tap water did little to rally my spirits. After gulping it down, I drove back into town and headed for the hospital.

Another day was crawling above the horizon. The steamy warm air that wafted through my open car window threatened far worse heat as the day matured. Summer in Alabama wasted little time.

12

Thursday Morning

I FOUND Dr. Hartley already well into his work in the morgue, even though the hour was just barely six. He had the look of a man who slept lightly and not well and I imagined that most mornings found him at work early, autopsy or no.

He inspected the naked body of Tommy Sheehy, who lay stretched out on the stainless steel table, stiff and bloody.

Hartley cast me a glance. "Anxious to get started today?"

"You and me both."

He grunted. "I like to get these out of the way while it's early. Nothing like a late afternoon postmortem to put you off dinner. What about you? This news isn't going to be any fresher now than at eight."

"What's it show?"

"Two bullet wounds in the chest, one in the mouth. Not pretty. Less professional than yesterday's. Fair amount of anger with this one, I'd say."

"It's a gruesome business, isn't it?"

He looked up at me. "I suppose. Murders and accidents have never really bothered me, though. I'd much rather do one of these than our in-hospital deaths."

"Really?"

"Yes," he said. "The evil that men do to each other is totally comprehensible. Bullets and broken bones are very clear in their mechanism of cause and effect."

"How is that easier?"

He stripped off his gloves and undid his rubber apron, hanging it carefully on a metal coat rack behind him.

"Come with me," he said.

I followed him into an adjoining office. He sat at the desk, rifled through a stack of papers and books, extracting finally a small, flat wooden box. He turned to a table that held a two-person microscope and motioned for me to sit.

I pulled up a chair opposite him at the microscope. He undid a small clasp on the wooden box and opened the hinged lid. The box contained a set of glass microscope slides neatly standing on end. He ruffled through the rows of slides until his fingers lit of the desired one. He mounted it on the microscope stage, fiddled with the light and focus, then motioned for me to look through my oculars.

I squinted through the eyepieces and saw a red and purple stained gobbet illuminated on the slide.

"This is a thin section from an unfortunate young woman. A section of brain. Notice the blue-staining area off to your left."

In the midst of a repetitive pattern of red lattice and blue macules, I saw a jumbled knot of deep blue. He centered the area under our gaze, swung the lens out of line so the field went dark, and placed a drop of oil from a small brown bottle onto the center of the slide. He swung a different lens into line and the field sprang back into view under the eyepieces, only now under higher power.

"What do you see?" he asked.

The nest of blue boiled and snaked upon itself, chaotic and jumbled.

"It's ugly," I said.

"Isn't it, though?" he said. "This is *glioblastoma multiforme*—a tumor, and a very ugly one. It killed this poor woman in short order. In the course of a few months she went from a healthy mother of two and leader of the Junior League to a collection of skin and bones fed through a tube down her nose. Death came quickly, yet not soon enough."

He raised his eyes from the microscope.

"*This* is gruesome," he said, gesturing toward the glass slide on the stage. "I can explain a gunshot wound or a shattered skull. I can't even begin to comprehend or explain this tumor. Look at it."

He turned back to the eyepieces.

"This is madness greater than any of man's follies and sins—this is madness within nature itself. We label it as a disease and distinguish it from that which we see in healthy tissue. But the distinction is groundless. The diseased tissue is as real and legitimate as the healthy. Nature harbors this madness at her very core. It is as much a part of her logic as respiration, mitosis, or enzyme function."

He spread his hands wide. "I cannot explain it," he said, "and it leads me to some rather unflattering conclusions about the benevolence and consideration of the Almighty."

I looked up at him.

"There is no requirement for *glioblastoma multiforme* in the divine plan," he went on. "There is no need for this aberration, and Creation would have been no less without it. Yet, there it is. . . ."

He lit another cigarette and sat back in his chair.

"Your father never got beyond bafflement over the evil of his fellow men. I never worried about that; it seemed a trivial and understandable problem."

"He was a romantic," I said.

"He was a sentimentalist. He had notions about how things ought to be and thought he could change them."

"Was he wrong?"

Hartley shook his head sadly. "You cannot change man. The madness springs from within. It's right here on this slide. It boils up from within us. Man is a beast at his core, and will sink to beastliness given the slightest encouragement."

FROM a pay phone in the hospital lobby I called The Watering Hole on the off chance I would catch someone in to comment on the murder, but there was no answer. I checked the telephone book, but found no listing for Tommy Sheehy.

I thumbed through my little black book. It was seven o'clock, eight in DC. I had a friend from my Richmond days who worked for the FBI in Washington. He, too, was an insomniac and a workaholic, so I dialed his office number, hoping I'd find him at work at this early hour.

"Edmonds," he said, picking up on the second ring.

"Jack!" I said, trying to sound like a long lost friend. "It's Nelson Ingram. How're you doing?"

"Nelson? Man, it's been years! Where the hell you been?"

He sounded happy to hear from me. Jack was a tall, imposing black man who originally hailed from Detroit. He had joined the FBI after Hoover died and the Bureau had finally begun to get past its white-bread image. I had known him when he worked in the Richmond field office. About the time my marriage was unwinding, he had gotten himself promoted to FBI headquarters in D.C.

"Here and there," I said. "Long story."

"What happened to you and that newspaper heiress?"

"Divorced, man. She finally figured out who I was."

"Sorry to hear that."

"Don't be."

"So, what's up?"

"Listen, I need a favor."

"What else is new?" he asked, laughing.

"I'm working down in Alabama on a newspaper. We've had a couple of murders in a couple of days and it's starting to smell fishy. The cops here are just sitting on their hands. I was wondering if you could run a couple of names through the computer for me?"

He hesitated for an instant, silently calculating in a mental ledger of debts and credits.

"Sure," he said, "I can run a few names."

I gave him the names and whatever personal information I had on Tommy Sheehy and Reginald Copley, then threw in the names of the two other murders from the last year, James Davidson and Isaiah Jackson. If I had known Malcolm's last name, I would have thrown him in too.

"Jesus," he said. "How many bodies you got down there?"

"Like I said, they're stacking up like cordwood and the cops are acting like the Three Stooges."

"I'll see what I can do. Do you have a fax number?"

I gave him the number at the paper.

"This'll take a while."

"Thanks, Jack. I owe you one."

"You owe me a few."

"I know. Maybe someday."

"Alabama? How the hell did you end up back there? That's the *Deep* South down there," he said, laughing.

"Man, I tell you, it's been a long, strange trip."

"I'll bet. Listen, I gotta go. Drop me a line and fill me in on things."

"Sure," I said.

"Yeah," he said and hung up.

I held the receiver of the pay phone to my ear for a moment, listening to the dead line then the disconnect and dial tone. I thought of Richmond and Mary Kate and felt suddenly lost. I would have given my right testicle for another chance with her. But she had given me a second and a third chance, and I had screwed them all up. All at once, I couldn't bring myself to care about anything.

I hung up the receiver and walked out to my car. The sun rose clear of the horizon and already pounded the day like a hammer on an anvil. Another day in hell.

I MADE the rounds of the sheriff's and police departments, but they were barren of any new information and their ignorance made them twice as defensive. There were no next of kin known for Sheehy. No one to contact. He was still just as dead.

I ate breakfast at Don's Biscuits 'n' Gravy out by the Interstate, thumbing through the Birmingham and Atlanta morning papers. The talk at the diner was of anything but these murders. Don shrugged amiably when I asked him if he was following the story and filled them in on Sheehy's murder. Dorothy, his wife and the waitress, just stared blankly. I gave up and tried to pull my notes together.

I had lots of suspicions, but precious few facts. Two bodies in two days. One victim was apparently a hardworking family man with an L.A. connection, the other an oily mob shark from up North doing god-knows-what down here. Malcolm looked like some latter-day Bobby Seal and exuded violence like a fog, but that was all I knew. It was not exactly enough to go to press with.

I paid the check then drove back to the *Ledger*. The best I could do was a couple of hundred words on the

Sheehy killing, referring to his background up North in a veiled fashion that left the reader to infer worse things. I knew that Leyland would probably ax that part, but if he was having a bad day, it might slip through.

The funeral for Reginald Copley was this afternoon. I planned to attend, but needed to run home to muster a more presentable facade for the occasion. I had grabbed my coat and was headed for the door when I ran into Leyland on his way in for the day.

He grunted a good-morning at the back of his throat, then reared back, looking down his nose, scrutinizing me.

"Look like somethin' the cat drug in, Ingram," he said.

"Long night," I said. "Another murder out in the county."

His eyes widened. "What are those *people* doing to each other?"

"This was a white man. Tommy Sheehy. Ran a saloon by the lake."

He looked aghast.

"Shot. Several times. Did you know him?"

He retreated into his patrician Southern uffishness. "Vaguely. Rotary Club."

"I see," I said, having a hard time seeing Tommy at a Rotary meeting except at gunpoint.

"You going to the dedication on the Tenn-Tom?" he asked, abruptly changing the subject.

My heart sank. The county commission had built an industrial park out on the Tennessee- Tombigbee Waterway in the vain hope of attracting industry to our godforsaken county, and today was its dedication. It was at two o'clock and the Copley funeral was at three-thirty. I would be hard pressed to attend both.

"Yessir," I told Leyland, "I'll be there."

"Good," he grunted. "And bring back more than you did from the Jaycees luncheon yesterday. Dig a little, boy."

I nodded. "Yessir."

On my way out the door, I ran into Connie coming in, looking not a bit worse for wear after her night out.

"Hey, Nelson," she said. She grabbed me by the arm. "Wasn't that terrible about Tommy?"

"Yeah. I got wind of it after I dropped you off. It wasn't pretty."

She shook her head. "Why would anyone want to do that to him?"

"Well, you said it yourself. He wasn't exactly a choirboy."

"I guess. But you never think of that kind of thing happening around here."

"Better get used to it," I said. "I think there's more to come."

Her eyes grew large and she turned her head to one side, unsure of how serious I was.

I HEADED straight for my car and dashed home. The sun had already climbed high in the sky and my little cabin sweltered under its bower of trees. I showered again in tepid well water and tried to dry off with the only towel I could find that did not reek of mildew. I dug through the closet and pulled out the dark summer-weight suit that Rayburn had bought me for my mother's funeral. On the way home I had stopped at Kmart and bought a white shirt. It felt scratchy and stiff. The collar chafed my freshly shaven neck. I pulled on the pants, knotted a sedate gray tie around my neck, then shrugged into the jacket.

Standing in front of the corroded bathroom mirror, I saw my father staring at me. I jumped backward and the specter jumped away too.

People had always said I resembled him, but I had never been able to see it. But now, there he was, staring at me out of my own face. The burning blue eyes under the shaggy brows, the despondent downturn of the lids, the dark circles beneath, the mouth pulled down into a perpetual frown. He had been forty when he died, and this was how I remembered him. This was how he had looked, laid out in the casket.

Lucille had stood with me by the casket, standing beside me, holding my shoulders between her hands.

"Look what a marvelous job Mr. Armstrong did," she said.

"You son of a bitch," I thought, "why did you leave me? Why didn't you care more about me and try harder to stay alive?" I tore myself away from Lucille and ran out of the funeral parlor.

Uncle Rayburn found me about a half-hour later, sitting under the big oak outside the library. I had taken my shoes and socks off and scratched lines in the dirt with a pointed stick I had whittled.

He stood beside me.

"Put your shoes on, Nelson," he said, "We're going to the cemetery for the service."

"You go on," I said. "I'll be along later." I felt surly and in no mood to be bossed by my uncle.

"Come on," he said. "You need to do this."

"What if I don't? You gonna send my pa out to whip me?"

He squatted in front of me, staring me in the eyes. "No, but *I'll* whip you. It's my place now."

"Why did he do it, Uncle Rayburn?" I asked him, tears suddenly streaming out. "Why did he kill himself like that?"

"He didn't do it on purpose, Nelson."

"He knew better! You knew better! Why'd you let him?"

I stood over him now, my fists balled up, fighting mad.

Rayburn grabbed me hard and pulled me close to him.

"It's done," he said. "There's no 'why' to it. It's done. Let it go."

I struggled in his grip for a moment, arms held out awkwardly, then anger again melted into tears. I wept and held on to him, no longer a man but a child again collapsing in the embrace of a grown-up. The world was too hard and confusing a place and I gave up trying to figure it out and just let Rayburn hold me, pretending that somehow things would be okay.

I TURNED from the mirror, went to the kitchen, poured two fingers of whiskey, and tossed it back, breaking my five o'clock pledge. My hands shook.

That son of a bitch knew better than to go hunting

when he'd drunk that much, knew better than to leave his safety off. He had stopped giving a damn about anything besides his own private despair; he had stopped trying to find a way out. And now here I was in his body and I'd never given a damn about anyone or anything except my own wretched, booze-loving self. I'd always been afraid to risk anything after losing him, and so I'd never let myself give a damn.

With another two fingers of whiskey, I erased any thought of suddenly growing a backbone at this late age. It burned all the way down. Soon its numbing effects would take hold and I would be able to exist again as a jellyfish in the unforgiving world.

13

Thursday Afternoon

THE industrial park on the Tennessee-Tombigbee Waterway lay at nearly the opposite end of the county from my cabin. Sweating a whiskey sweat in the midday swelter, I drove south and west down a patchwork of two-lane highways. The Tenn-Tom was a creation of the Army Corps of Engineers and powerful interests in Tennessee, Mississippi, and Alabama. Their will had been given shape by senators and congressmen from these states wielding a suffocating seniority over the great pork barrel that is federal appropriations for inland waterways. A series of canals linked the Tennessee River with the Tombigbee River and thence south to its confluence with the Alabama River, and from there via the Mobile River to Mobile Bay and the

Gulf of Mexico. Our own little Sour Mash River was a minor tributary to the Alabama.

There was no particular need for the waterway, and most studies done before the project showed it to be at least a giant irrelevancy and, at worst, an environmental disaster. Yet men with interests in shipping and transportation and public works conceived of it as a great ribbon of water draining the Southeast as the Mississippi does the Midwest, a conduit for commerce transforming Mobile into another New Orleans—a great port city linked to the world.

God only knows how much money was made off the rights-of-way and the padded contracts for the work. The whole thing finally opened in 1985 to a great fanfare and all stood back and waited for the Silent Hand of the Market to transform it into a throbbing liquid highway of commerce. Sadly, little happened. A few barges chugged up and down the channels, coal and cotton and tobacco moving north and south, but mostly the waterway sat empty.

Probably every small town whose path the waterway crossed had harbored dreams of becoming a pulsing boomtown on the banks of the New Mississippi, and most every small town had been sorely disappointed. Litchfield was no different. The only thing that had come so far was the dog track, thrown up on a lot along the waterway because they thought flowing water leant a more recreational air to the place. Throwing good money after bad, the county commission had seen fit to lay out an ambitious industrial park—several large parcels of land with roads and utilities brought in at taxpayer expense to entice who-knows-what corporation into relocating from up North. So far, there had been a few lookers but no takers.

Now, on this sticky late spring afternoon, a small cluster of people gathered for the public dedication of the industrial park. A flatbed truck served as the speakers' platform, with a couple of dozen folding chairs arranged around its back end in a semicircle.

I parked, got out, and began to work the crowd. Most of the attendees, it turned out, were family members of the county commissioners, brought in to create the illusion of interest. I pumped the commissioners for some quotable remarks, then did the same with whatever other local figures I could identify. Rumors ran rampant. The Japanese were looking to use Litchfield as a distribution point, lugging Toyotas up the Tenn-Tom for all of the Deep South between New Orleans and Jacksonville. In another version, it was the Germans looking to do the same for their Mercedes Benzes or BMWs. General Foods was looking at the site for a sugar refinery. Or was it General Motors and a parts distribution hub? Several people had it on good authority that JVC was interested in a plant to manufacture videotape. On and on it went, and after a while I got the feeling that no one really believed any of it—a collective and willing suspension of disbelief keeping the whole hopeful dream afloat.

In fact, no one could really believe that anything good would ever happen in Potter County, for nothing ever had. The Civil War had not even had the decency to come through town, sparing the county of even a drop of bloodshed and depriving them of whatever grievance and dignity a storied visitation by Grant or

Sherman might have provided. A tire plant, put up by Goodyear during the Korean War, had limped into the seventies only to expire during one of its recessions. A paper mill had eked out a modest trade until the early eighties when the EPA drove them into bankruptcy over their polluting of the upper Sour Mash. Litchfield was used to an obscure rural poverty, inculcated over two centuries. So, the people here spoke bravely of change, but no one really believed it would ever happen.

The dedication ceremony itself was blessedly brief. The chairman of the county commission made a few laudatory, self-congratulatory comments, then the head of the chamber of commerce did the same. The homecoming queen of Litchfield High cut a red ribbon strung across the entrance to the otherwise vacant industrial park. The *Ledger*'s photographer, a freelancer from the university, snapped a few photos. The whole thing was over by three o'clock.

I dashed back to the car and headed back across the county toward Banfield, hoping to get there in time for the Copley funeral.

THE oaks that peopled the cemetery were well beyond a hundred years old—great thick-trunked trees with generous canopies of leaves that shaded most of the grounds. Gravestones dated from the 1840s onward, most of the markers simple and unadorned. This was not a rich man's cemetery, and held mainly the poor black folk of Banfield. A group of twenty or thirty gathered in the far corner around an open plot, beside which sat a simple casket.

I had parked out behind the grounds, and tried to approach from the rear, without drawing undue attention—a difficult thing to do when you are the only white face in a crowd that is not in a very charitable state toward people of my color. I caught more than a few over-the-shoulder glares, and the preacher, who faced the gathering and had a full view of my advance, held me in a pitiless gaze for many moments.

I straightened my tie, buttoned my suit jacket, took out my notepad, and tried to look humble and journalistic.

The ceremony was almost finished. The preacher went on about the tragedy of young life lost and the inscrutability of God's plan. I scanned the crowd from behind. I picked out Malcolm's shaved head and black leather jacket, and then located Latoya, holding the baby in her arms. She rocked the baby gently and seemed to be whispering to him. Heads bowed in prayer, murmuring a tract I did not know, ending in a vigorous Amen.

The crowd began to break up, some drifting back toward their cars, others gathering around the widow and mother to offer condolences. I remained in the background, standing beside one of the oaks. Latoya looked up and I caught her eye. Whispering again to her baby, she kissed him on the forehead and gave him to someone beside her. She sifted out of the crowd toward me.

"What do you want here?" she asked, standing opposite me, but keeping the oak half between us.

"Just trying to get to the bottom of things," I said.

"You found out who killed my Reggie?"

"No, but I'm still looking. There was a man killed

last night—a white man named Tommy Sheehy. That name mean anything to you?"

She shook her head. "Don't know no white folks around here."

"I saw Malcolm with him a few hours before he died."

"I don't have no say about what Malcolm does."

"What's Malcolm doing out here?"

"Don't know his business. Don't wanna know."

She scooted closer to me, still hugging the trunk of the oak.

"Don't mess with him," she hissed at me. "He'd as soon kill you as piss on you. *I'm* scared of him and I'm his sister. You oughta be scared stupid of him."

"Well, isn't this fuckin' cute?" a deep voice asked from behind me. Malcolm had come up from my blind side, and now stood behind me, looming like bad weather.

"We just talking," his sister said. "About Reggie."

I turned and took a step away from him.

"I told you to stay out of this, white boy," he said, worrying a toothpick between his teeth. He stared at me in his unfocused, malevolent way.

"Look," I said, "I'm just doing my job. I'm just going to file a story on the funeral." I pulled out my notepad. "If you'd like to make any comments, I'd be happy to print them."

This threw him off for half a beat, enticed by the notion of media fame, however limited. But he quickly dismissed the thought. He snatched the notepad from my hands and tore it in half.

"Stay out of my fuckin' way, cracker," he said, scattering the torn pages.

He pushed past me, knocking me back with his shoulder.

I leapt after the scattered pages. They contained all my notes for the last few days. Latoya bent down to help.

"He's got something going down tonight," she whispered to me. "He's cranked up and tight as a spring."

"Where?"

"I don't know," she said. "Somewhere out at the lake. I don't want to know any more than that."

"What time?"

"Late."

I slipped her one of my business cards. "Call me if you learn anything more. Reggie's death might have something to do with this."

"You think I don't know that? Reggie was clean. Malcolm didn't do it. But something happened and Malcolm's been breathing fire ever since."

I stood with the torn pages of my notes. She handed me the few she had retrieved.

"Thanks," I said.

She slipped the business card into her purse.

"Don't cross Malcolm," she said. "He stone scary and he's just looking for a reason to cap some white ass."

14

Thursday Afternoon

BACK at the office, I found the fax from Jack Edmonds, bearing an impressive FBI seal on the cover sheet, sitting on my desk.

Edmonds had been busy since we spoke. There was almost nothing on Reginald Copley—a couple of traffic violations from Birmingham in the early eighties, a single misdemeanor marijuana charge from L.A. two years ago, nothing more. James Davidson, the young man killed last November, had a more interesting story. He had a long rap sheet from L.A., including assaults, B&E's, and possession and felony trafficking charges. He had spent time in San Quentin. The victim for last June, Isaiah Jackson, had a sheet that was similar to Davidson's—multiple busts, time served.

Tommy Sheehy's sheet was the jackpot. Jack had included a detailed report. Born Thomas Ignatius Sheehy in 1948 in Litchfield, Alabama, drafted into the U.S. Army in 1968. He did a tour of duty in Vietnam and was suspected of being involved in heroin trafficking out of the Golden Triangle. Little detail on this, but it led to a dishonorable discharge in 1969. He surfaced again in Detroit in 1970, suspected of trafficking in cocaine and heroin. Convicted in 1972 of cocaine trafficking, he spent eight years in the federal penitentiaries before being released on parole. He was invisible to the system for about five years—the duration of his parole. He resurfaced briefly in Detroit and then appeared back down here in Litchfield running an up-and-up restaurant and bar.

But Edmonds had dug a little deeper. The Watering Hole was owned by a subsidiary of Burmington Southern Corp. Among its other holdings were textile mills in Central America, a shipping and transport company based in Mobile; large tracts of timber land throughout Alabama, Mississippi, and Tennessee; several paper mills; and a series of horse and dog tracks, including GreenDowns Dog Track here in Litchfield. The company's ownership was difficult to elucidate, lost in a series of offshore holding companies. I got the sense of connections here lying just out of reach, as if one or two more pieces of information would pull the whole thing into a coherent picture.

I telephoned Riley Hill out at the dog track, having to wade through two obstructionist secretaries before finally getting the man himself. I introduced myself and told him the paper was interested in a promotional piece about the track. He brightened at the prospect of free publicity and agreed to meet me at the track offices at five o'clock.

I checked my watch. It was past four-thirty. I had missed my afternoon meeting with Rayburn, had missed the afternoon deadline for the paper, hadn't written a word for tomorrow's stories, hadn't had two hours' sleep in two days, and would probably be up all night trying to stake out Lake Litchfield to track whatever was going down with Malcolm. A sticky sweat of caffeine and whiskey and fatigue clung to me. My stomach rumbled. My back ached; my knees complained arthritically as I stood. I was getting too old for this nonsense.

Connie came into the room from the stairs.

"Hey, Nelson," she said.

"Hey," I said, feeling awkward.

She sidled up to my desk. "What'cha working on?" she asked coyly. She picked up the faxed rap sheets.

"Goddamn, Nelson," she said. "I always thought the stuff they said about Tommy was just gossip."

"That's not the half of it," I said, and filled her in on what I'd learned. Three young black men had been killed under fishy circumstances in the last year. Malcolm, the brother-in-law of the last victim and a hostile dude from L.A. of unknown but dangerous intentions, appears to be planning something tonight on Lake Litchfield. He's seen talking pointedly to Tommy Sheehy, a local boy with serious mob ties. Mr. Sheehy turns up dead later that same night. The company that owns the dog track turns out to be a huge corporation that also coincidentally owns the bar that Sheehy managed. I told her I was on my way to interview Riley Hill and see what I could see.

"Can I go with you?" she asked excitedly.

"I don't know—"

She cut me off. "Oh, please, Nelson. Please. You don't know how boring it is here around the office. I'd do anything to help you with this story."

"Okay," I said, not equal to arguing with her.

"Thank you, thank you," she said, hugging me around the neck. "You won't be sorry."

I locked up my desk and we headed for the door.

"You think maybe I could share a byline with you?"

"I think we're getting ahead of ourselves."

I DROPPED Connie off at the dog track's lounge to "check things out," while I went on to the track's administrative offices. I gave my name to Riley Hill's secretary and she buzzed through to him.

Riley came out promptly and welcomed me into his office with a gesture toward a chair that stood opposite his desk. He rocked back and forth behind his desk, regarding me impassively, giving away little behind a facade of bovine simplicity. Air whistled through congested nasal passages. His office was large and plush, a picture window looking out on the grandstands and track.

"So kind of you to see me on such short notice," I said.

"What can I do for you, Mr. Ingram?" he asked in his drawn-out backwoods accent.

"Well, we have some space in our Saturday supplements for next month, and we're thinking a series of pieces about the track might be timely. It's been a while since y'all had any local publicity," I said, drawling right back at him.

He raised an eyebrow. "Y'all just ran a piece three months ago."

I winced inwardly. I should have skimmed the back issues of the paper before I opened my mouth and put my foot in it. Riley was backwoods Clay Mountain white trash, and about as swift with most things as molasses in January, but his years on the farm had left him with a decent ability to smell bullshit when it was presented to him.

"Well," I said, stalling now for time, "I was thinking about a different angle, not just another glossy tourist piece, but maybe a character piece on all the different personalities at the track—you know, the players, the regulars, the trainers, the jockeys. . . ."

"This is a dog track, Mr. Ingram. We don't have no jockeys."

Strike two.

"I'm sorry, I was getting carried away. But you know what I mean—"

He looked at his watch.

"I suppose. Why don't you set up some days to hang around the track. I'll introduce you around, you can meet some of our more colorful *characters*."

He stood, signaling it was time for me to leave. I stood with him, but let him come from around his desk and walk me slowly to the door.

"Thank you much for your time," I said, gushing, and pumping his hand.

"No problem, Mr. Ingram."

"I hope business is good," I said.

"Oh, yes. Attendance is up twenty percent from last year. Got a new set of TV ads running statewide and in eastern Mississippi."

"Oh, I saw those. Those are too much!"

"We like 'em." He turned me to the door.

"Oh, I just had one more question," I said, turning my back on the door to face him again.

"What's that?"

"Now, GreenDowns is owned by the Burmington Southern Corporation, is that right?"

He smiled, confused at the sudden change in course. "That's right."

"Were you aware that they also owned a drinking establishment out by Lake Litchfield?"

He cast his eyes about, trying to get his bearings. "Why, no, I wasn't aware of that."

"And that the manager of that establishment was murdered last night?"

He focused in on me. "No, I hadn't heard that."

I stared at him for a beat, letting silence hang between us. He was unsure as to what was going on.

"Were you aware that Mr. Sheehy had ties to organized crime in the Midwest?"

His temper flared. "Listen to me, Tommy Sheehy was a good man—"

"So you did know Mr. Sheehy? And had you heard of what happened last night?"

He bit back on his anger. "It's time for you to go," he said, opening the door and shepherding me out firmly.

He waved to his secretary. "See that Mr. Ingram finds his way out."

The secretary rose and came forward. I turned once again to face Riley.

"What are you trying to cover up?"

"We'll cover you up if you don't watch yourself," he said and slid back into his office, slamming the door behind him.

His secretary was at my side, taking my arm in a crushing grip.

"This way, Mr. Ingram," she said.

I went docilely, finding myself standing outside, shocked by the transition from the arctic cool of the offices to the suffocating late afternoon heat. The sun hit me straight in the face, still high in the west, the air thick and humid. Black as a nightmare, clouds huddled up from the south, the white crown of a thunderhead piling high into the stratosphere. Except for a rumble of thunder, all seemed deathly quiet.

The GreenDowns lounge beckoned, a neon Budweiser logo glowing in the dark window.

The lounge offered a generic but welcome quiet. Rows of liquor bottles glittered behind the bar. The crowd was light and anonymous, huddled into booths along the walls. Muzak filtered through the air.

Connie waited for me at the bar opposite the door. I sat down next to her.

A young bartender in a pressed white shirt, bow tie, and red striped vest smiled at my approach.

"What can I get for you today?" he asked pleasantly, deferential and friendly, couth in visage and well spoken. He was the very antithesis of my favorite bartender, the anti-Jerome. If they were ever to meet, a tremendous explosion would ensue as matter and anti-matter annihilated each other.

"A beer," I said. "Bud draft."

He nodded smartly.

"So, what did you get from Riley?" Connie asked.

"Denials and obfuscation. Enough to confirm that there's something here that stinks."

The beer appeared in an iced glass, centered on a Budweiser coaster, a napkin and a bowl of pretzels beside it.

"So, what's next, chief?" she asked.

"Please. Don't call me chief."

"Sorry. It's just that this all seems so . . . dramatic."

"Yeah, well, I still don't have anything besides a bunch of suspicions."

"So what do we do next?"

"I've got to figure out how to find out what this Malcolm is up to out at the lake tonight."

She pondered, swirling the ice around in her drink. "If something is going down at the lake, it's probably going down at the north end, as far from town as possible."

"Maybe."

"I know a high place on the upper half of the lake," she said. "You sit up there with a pair of binoculars, you might be able to see a couple miles in either direction."

"Yeah?" I said. "Tell me more."

"My ex-brother-in-law's a soldier-of-fortune nut. Runs around in the woods on the weekends with his buddies fighting Russians and liberals. He's got some night vision binoculars. He'd probably let me borrow them."

"This is sounding better all the time," I said.

She drained her whiskey. "This sounds like fun," she said.

"You see what you can round up," I said. "We'll touch base at about eight o'clock tonight."

She picked up her purse. "I love this," she said. "Let's get on it."

I left a ten for the drinks and we went back out into the furnace of the afternoon.

15

Thursday Evening

NIGHT found me on a bluff above Lake Litchfield, sitting beside Connie on the trunk of my car, staring out at the lake, wondering just what I was looking for. The air hung close and warm, the surrounding woods thrummed with life. Mosquitoes buzzed lazily, occasionally choosing to alight on a bare arm or neck despite the generous layers of Cutters that we had applied. My stiff new Levi's dug in behind my knees and into my crotch.

Connie reached into her ice chest and pulled out a couple of beers. I twisted off the tops and handed her one.

"If this second date is any measure, I'd say this relationship is going downhill fast," she said.

"After this I just flop on the sofa at your house and watch TV," I said.

My new T-shirt caused a terrible itching up and down my back and chest. I had brought few clothes and no jeans with me when I returned to Litchfield. My entire wardrobe consisted of the undertaker's suit that Rayburn had bought for me, three pairs of worn khakis, an assortment of button-down shirts, and enough underwear and socks to allow me to go two weeks between runs to the laundromat. For this rustic expedition, I had to run into Kmart and buy a pair of black Levi's, a dark T-shirt, and a cheap pair of Nikes. Then, before meeting Connie, I had run back over to the newspaper offices and hacked up some copy for the next day's edition, including the stories on the Industrial Park opening, the Copley funeral, and what I had learned about Sheehy. This last piece I worked the longest on, although I knew it was most likely to be killed by Leyland.

A yellow moon a little past full crawled up over the hills to the east. The storm that had threatened all afternoon still sat off to the south, rumbling and flashing. Connie and I quibbled back and forth, half in play, half serious, killing time. An hour passed, then another.

"Just what are we looking for?" she asked.

"I don't know. Something. They're using the lake for a rendezvous, so I'm guessing that means boats."

She scanned the lake with the night vision binoculars. "Haven't seen anyone out there for at least half an hour and nothing suspicious at all. If something doesn't give soon, I'm packing it in."

"Be patient," I said. "Folks like this Malcolm don't even get out of bed until noon. Their juices don't really get flowing until ten or so at night."

"What's that?" Connie asked, pointing to the south.

Out of the south, against the dark of the storm I could see a pair of lights coming in at treetop level. Connie was on it with the binoculars.

"Wing lights," she said. "It's a small plane."

She handed the binoculars to me. The wing lights and cockpit glowed brightly, the rest of the plane in shadows.

"It's got pontoons. It's a seaplane," I said.

It swooped down over the tree-covered hills and down into the flooded river valley that was Litchfield Lake, hugging the ground the whole way.

"He's got to have night vision equipment to fly like that," I said.

The plane flew up the lake, around a bend obscured from us by the shoulder of a hill, and then reappeared farther up the lake. I zoomed in with the glasses. The cockpit glowed and I could make out a couple of shapes. The pontoons cut into the water, sending up a linear spray, and the plane settled into the water and slowed. It taxied farther up the lake, receding from us, then turned toward the near shore.

"They're up past Runner's Landing," she said.

She walked over to the passenger side of the car, grabbing a county map off the seat. Coming back to the trunk, she unfolded it, shining a flashlight down.

"The landing's flooded now by the lake, but the road still runs out to the edge of the water. There's a boat ramp there now." She studied the map. "We could drive down this road. It'll bring us in upriver from the landing."

"You up for it?" I asked. "We don't have any idea what we're getting into."

"I ain't come this far to turn back."

• • •

WE coasted down the last fifty yards of Live Oak Road, engine and lights off, rolling to a stop against one shoulder just short of the lakefront. We sat for a moment, windows down, listening. The wind had picked up and rustled through the leaves of the trees, crashing through the branches high in the canopy of the woods.

Connie slowly snapped open her door and I slid out after her. I knelt at the edge of the woods and trained the night vision glasses through the trees toward Runner's Landing. I could see nothing through the crisscross of tree trunks.

"I'm going in closer," I whispered to Connie.

She nodded and we crept single file between the trees, moving slowly, choosing our footing carefully. Thunder boomed close by now and the wind tore at the treetops.

Twenty yards into the woods I stopped again and checked through the glasses. I thought I could see silhouettes shimmering in and out of focus behind the trees. I made out two vehicles. Three or four men trooped back and forth, carrying what looked like boxes or bundles up from the shore to their cars.

Lightning and thunder came close upon one another, illuminating the woods in a flash of blue followed by a resounding crack. The figures stood in the open road, suddenly plain to see. I pulled myself down and behind a tree trunk. Darkness descended again and for an instant the roaring of the woods fell to silence.

"Shit," I heard one of them say.

Another stroke of lightning strobed blue, the thunder booming half a second behind.

"If they don't kill us, this storm's gonna," Connie hissed at me. "Ain't you seen enough?"

There was another loud report. Something in my gut told me to get low. I pulled Connie down beside me. A series of sharp reports came close after.

"Shit, that's gunfire. Automatic weapons."

"They saw us," Connie cried.

I peered around the tree trunk. Short barrel automatic weapons barked. But the muzzle flashes came from far up the road. The men unloading the plane scattered and ducked for cover, dropping their bundles. I heard cries and screams, only to be lost in another blast of thunder. The muzzle flashes strobed silently now in the blue-white lightning and roar of thunder.

Darkness swallowed them again. I swung the binoculars up. Six or eight men moved down the road, firing in short bursts first in one direction then another. Voices cried out at first, but one by one were silenced.

I crept forward a little, still peering through the glasses. Bodies lay all around.

"What the hell's happening?" Connie hissed.

"Quiet. Just lay low and pray they don't know we're here."

One man got on a walkie-talkie. A van rolled down the road. They opened the side door and pulled out body bags. They bagged the bodies and slung them into the van.

Rain began to spatter the treetops and land heavily on the ground around us.

I heard the sound of a scuffle. They pulled a man out of the brush. He struggled with them, cursing. I focused in with the glasses. It looked like Malcolm. He spat and fought. They clubbed him across the back of the head and threw him into the back seat of one of the cars.

One of the men stood down by the seaplane. He seemed to be talking amiably with the pilot, who waded in the shallows inspecting the plane for damage. The bundles were loaded again back on the plane. The seaplane motor cranked over and its lights came on. They waved at him and the plane turned and taxied down the lake, the pitch of its engine rising as it gained speed and moved away.

It looked like the whole thing had been setup with the pilot being in on it. The two cars and van started up, the headlights came on, illuminating the road, and they all sped away. In a moment, everything was gone.

We squatted for a few minutes in the woods, rain falling all about us.

"Let's go check out the scene," I said.

We crept forward toward the edge of the road clearing. The rain fell heavily now. The clearing was deserted.

I stepped out into the road. The blood was being rapidly washed away by the rain, the shell casings of the spent rounds covered up by the rivulets of silt running down the road to the lake. Men had just died here, but there was almost no sign of it.

"Let's go before we drown," I said.

16

Friday Morning

WE drove back through the downpour, dripping wet, the windows steaming up.

"Jesus, Nelson," Connie said. "Those were killers! They would've killed us just for breathing!"

"Sorry. Didn't know it would turn out that way." I reached into my glove box and pulled out a hip flask.

"Just what was that?" she asked, taking the flask from me and tossing some back.

"Some bad shit," I said. My hands still shook, my heart thumped in my chest. She handed the flask to me. I nipped at the whiskey.

"So what do we do now?" she asked.

"There was one survivor," I said. "They took him with them. It looked like that Malcolm fellow I told you about."

"Yeah, but took him where?" she asked, taking the flask back and tossing back another shot.

I thought for a moment, feeling the whiskey smolder in my gut.

"Turn left up ahead," I said. "I've got a hunch."

She whooped. "God, this is fun!"

WE pulled up a quarter mile short of The Watering Hole, running with the lights out for the last mile and coasting the last hundred yards with the engine off. The rain had blown over. The clouds had pushed off to the north. The moon hung high in the sky, the stars twinkling through air scrubbed clean of the summer funk. The woods dripped and rustled. I rolled the car off the road and under the cover of a large oak.

A pasture separated The Watering Hole from the road. The electric sign was off, the parking lot holding only a couple of cars illuminated by a single floodlight on the roof.

"What now?" Connie asked.

"Wait here," I said. "Watch me with the glasses. If you see trouble coming, honk your horn once then get the hell out. I'll cut across the woods and look for you down on the highway."

"What are you going to do?"

"See what there is to see."

"Listen," she said, "these men are killers. Maybe we should just go into town and have a drink."

"Just wait here."

I popped open the door. The dome light came on and

I felt like a deer caught in the headlights of an oncoming car.

"Shit," I said, and quickly pushed the door shut after me.

I cut up the road to where the fence line of the pasture ran alongside the neighboring woods. Once there, I stole from the woods on the edge of the road over to the woods running along the fence. I followed the fence into the pasture until I faced the back of The Watering Hole. I paused for a moment, listening. All was quiet. I took a deep breath and made my way quickly across the pasture in a crouch.

Years of sloth had left me in miserable condition and my rapid trot slowed to a dignified walk by the time I made it across the pasture and crept into the shadows on the backside to the building. The wall was cinder block, cool and damp to the touch. I squatted down, my back to it, in the shadow of a Dumpster, listening to the hum of the woods and the whirring of the air conditioners. Two windows off to my left cast a latticed light.

I stood and moved slowly down the wall toward the lighted window. Venetian blinds covered it, but the slats were only half-closed. Peering between the slats, I could make out a bare room illuminated by incandescent light. In the middle of the room, a man sat in a chair with his back to me, his hands bound around the back of the chair, his head slumped forward.

It was an aluminum-framed sliding window. I eased my pocket knife along the leading edge of it to pry it open a half an inch so I could hear what was going on inside. The window protested then slid open with a muted rumble.

My heart pounded in my chest. This was crazy. It was going to get me killed.

Two men entered the room. They stood facing the man slumped in the chair. I craned my ear near the crack in the window to listen.

"See, I told ya," one of them said. "He's dead."

The other bent over the man in the chair for a minute.

"Shit, Lenny," he said at last. "First you kill the wrong nigger, then you let this one die when we wanted him alive."

"He was gut shot already," Lenny said.

The other lifted up the head of the man tied to the chair. His head lolled from side to side. It looked like Malcolm, bald and bloodied.

"Shit," he said disgustedly. He let the head drop. "Get rid of this."

"Sure," Lenny said.

"Didn't he have a wife?"

"A sister. She's got a kid, too. And a mother-in-law. There's a houseful of 'em."

"Go pick them up when you get through here. We can't leave any loose ends."

Lenny untied the hands and settled the body into an open body bag on the floor.

I turned and crept back across the pasture, then along the woods back to the car.

"WHAT?" Connie shouted as I drove the car back down the road in big hurry.

"We have to go get the Copleys," I told her. "They're

going to nab them. There's no police in Banfield and God knows how long the sheriff would take to get out there."

"Now this is goin' too far, Nelson," she said. "I already risked getting my butt shot once tonight, I ain't going to do it twice."

"Fine," I said. "I can't ask you to do any more than you've done already. Your house is on the way to Banfield anyway. I'll go by myself."

"You're crazy, Nelson," she said. "Risk getting your ass shot off for a newspaper story."

"I'll drop you off. It's okay."

"This isn't for you to do," she said. "Let's just go to my house and call the sheriff."

"No, I've got to do this," I said.

"You don't know the half of what's going on here," she said. "Just come home with me and we'll call for help." She reached out and brushed my hair.

I pulled away from her. "I've got to do this," I said.

My heart still pounded. If I had half a brain, I'd have listened to her and steered clear of this. It *was* crazy, it *was* stupid to be hanging my ass out there for a story for a shitty little newspaper in a backwater town, crazy to be driving to the rescue of a woman I did not even know who would probably shoot me on sight. But this woman and her baby had done nothing to hurt anyone and were caught up now in God knows what and they needed help. There seemed to be a momentum and logic to the events. Things needed witnessing and doing, and there was no one else to do them. I had spent my whole life running from things and shirking duty, and now here I was with events calling on me to act and feeling myself able to act, and goddamnit but I wasn't going to stop just because I was scared.

The car's engine roared. I found myself grinning like a wolf and breathing great lungfuls of air through the open window.

17

Friday Morning

I ROLLED up to the Copley house and honked the horn. Leaving the engine running, I jumped out and took the front steps of the house three at a time. I leaned on the doorbell and rapped hard on the door with the other hand.

After a moment the porch light snapped on and curtains beside the door parted.

"Who's there?" someone called from behind the door—an older woman's voice.

"It's Nelson Ingram from the newspaper." I said. "It's urgent that we talk."

"It's two in the morning," she said.

"Ma'am," I shouted through the closed door, "Malcolm's been killed. Murdered. There are men coming to take you all away. Bad men. It's urgent that you leave with me now."

The door cracked open. Old Mrs. Copley stared at me. In the porch light I could see her eyes were wide and fearful.

"You've got to trust me, ma'am," I said, meeting her eyes. "There's no time to waste."

She pushed the door to, rattled loose the chain, then opened it wide. I stepped inside.

The living room light came on. Latoya crouched behind an overstuffed chair pointing a 9mm at my chest.

"What's your part in this mess?" she asked. "And remember, I can shoot this thing."

The gun trembled in her grip and her eyes were just as wide as Mrs. Copley's. The cries of the baby came from a back room.

"I'm just caught in the middle," I said. "Honest. I followed Malcolm to his pickup point and he and his people got massacred. The men who killed them are coming after you. That's all I know. And the longer we stand around here, talking, the closer they get."

She stared at me for a long minute—and a minute with someone pointing a gun at you is a very long time. Finally she clicked the safety on the pistol and lowered it.

"Let's go," I said. "Now. No time to grab anything. Just get the baby and let's go. You too, Mrs. Copley."

They both nodded meekly, too scared to argue.

Mrs. Copley got in the backseat of my car, holding the baby, while Latoya climbed in front. In another minute, we were gone.

I drove back to the cabin. The baby fussed for a few

minutes then settled in to the rocking of the car and fell asleep. Latoya sat cradling the pistol in her lap.

"You want to tell me what the hell's going on here?" I asked.

She sat in silence for a while, probably deciding what she would tell me.

"Malcolm was a crazy muther," she said. "I met Reggie in L.A. three years ago. When I got pregnant with Little Reggie, he married me and we moved here. To get away from the drugs and the gangs and the shootings. Malcolm came to visit. There ain't much in the way of drugs around here. He saw it as an *opportunity*. To open up his own gig. He got the blessing from the Crips and was gonna use their connections to get something going. He thought he'd try to start dealing crack into all the little towns between Birmingham and Jackson. Pay the Crips a cut. Reggie and me told him not to do it, but he didn't listen."

"What was he thinking about? Folks in the black community don't have two dimes to rub together. Where did he think money for drugs was going to come from?"

"Oh, man. There's always money for crack once you get a taste of it. Besides, Malcolm was gonna deal to all the white boys. Get all these cracker teenagers and make 'em crackheads. Crackerheads, he called 'em. Thought that was so damn funny. Wanted to go to the university and start selling to the college boys, too."

"Big plans." It still didn't make sense why mobsters would care about an L.A. lone wolf trying to run drugs in this lost corner of the world.

"I don't think the homies back in Compton thought

much of it," she said. "Everyone was just going along. Showed up here coked out of his brain waving pistols around. Malcolm's always been looking for a way to get his piece of the pie. He said this was gonna be his time. Then they grabbed Reggie. . . ."

"I think they grabbed Reggie by mistake," I said.

"Yeah. All us niggers look alike."

"Who are these men who killed them?"

"I don't know. I wish I knew who they were. Cracker sons of bitches." Her voice broke and she began to cry. "They killed my Reggie and he didn't do nothing wrong."

"I'm sorry," I said.

"I'm so scared," she said. "What am I gonna do?"

"It's going to be all right," I said. It was just what Rayburn had said to me all those years ago when my father had died and things were anything but okay. It is amazing what comfort can be taken from empty promises.

We drove for a while in silence.

"What you gonna do with us?" she asked finally.

I had thought about bringing them to stay with Rayburn and Lucille, but a black woman with a baby in that neighborhood would quickly garner attention. I considered doing it anyway just to see the look on Lucille's face as I trooped the three of them into her sitting room in the dead of night. Finally, I decided it was wiser to let them stay at the cabin.

"I've got a place you all can stay. It'll be safe for a few days until we figure out what to do next."

• • •

LATOYA looked less than enthused as we walked up the steps and into the cabin, but Mrs. Copley marched in like it was home.

"That couch a pullout?" she asked.

"Yes, ma'am," I said. "There are two bedrooms and I'll take the couch. I'm sorry there's no air conditioning, but all the windows open and have tight screens, so it gets pretty airy in here at night."

Latoya sat down on the sofa, holding Little Reggie like a drowning person holding on to a raft. She stared about the place glumly. The baby slept soundly, not seeming to care about all the commotion.

"I can run to the Winn-Dixie and get some supplies," I said as Mrs. Copley pulled open the refrigerator and stared at its cavernous emptiness. "What do you need? Milk? Bread?"

Mrs. Copley pulled a note pad out from her purse and began scribbling, looking through the cabinets and fridge.

"You got grits anywhere?" she asked.

"Just these," I said, pulling out a box of quick grits in a crumbling paper container that probably dated from the Kennedy Administration. As I lifted it, the bottom fell out and a cascade of ancient mealy grits settled onto the counter top.

"I'll clean that up," she said. "Get regular grits. And we need a big thing of disposable diapers." She handed me a long list of items.

"Pampers," Latoya said. "The extra-absorbent kind. Fifteen- to twenty-one-pound size."

I added that to the list. "When I come back down that road, I'll honk my horn twice as I do it. Anyone else comes, y'all kill the lights, call 911, and hunker down with that gun in the back bedroom."

Mrs. Copley came back from the pantry.

"You need a new broom," she said, holding up the scraggly veteran I had been using.

I nodded and headed down to the car.

AT four in the morning a strange assortment of people inhabit all-night grocery stores—insomniacs pushing carts along, rumpled middle-aged men drifting through after the bars have closed, early risers already dressed and headed out to daybreak jobs. I wandered the aisles, list in hand, pushing the shopping cart, boggling at how vivid all the items on the shelves seemed under the bright fluorescent lights.

All the while, I was also struggling to put together what had happened. Seven bodies in three days. Guns, drugs, gangs, the mob—all in Potter County, where nothing had happened since the end of the Civil War. And how had this sprung up almost overnight? And why did anyone care enough about drugs in Litchfield to leave all these bodies behind them? Drug arrests were a rare thing in the police logs, and not even a whisper was heard of any large-scale distribution locally. There seemed to be a part of the picture missing.

In such an addled state, it took me close to an hour to make my way through the grocery store. By the time I checked out, it was past five and the first gray stain of dawn had begun to creep up the eastern sky.

Standing in the parking lot, loading the bags into the

trunk, still damp and itchy in my rain-soaked clothes, I had a sudden hunch.

I slammed the trunk closed and walked to a pay phone outside of the Winn-Dixie. I found the number of The Watering Hole in the phone book, fished a quarter out of my pocket, and dialed. It rang a half a dozen times before someone answered.

"Yeah." A man's voice, full of annoyance.

"Lenny?" I said, taking a chance.

"Who the fuck is this?"

"Lenny, let me talk to your boss."

"Who the fuck is this?"

"Listen to me, Lenny. You don't know me from Adam, but I know you and I know what you've done and I know what you're up to. I've got the girl and the baby. Now can I talk to your boss?"

"Fuck you!"

"Five bodies tonight, Lenny," I said, looking around the parking lot, hoping no one else was within earshot. "Five bodies. The last one died in the back room of the place you're standing in right now. You think you got all the blood cleaned up? Think again, dumbshit. I call the cops and they'll be all over you and your boss like a cheap suit before the sun breaks the horizon."

There was silence on the other end of the line.

"Hold on a minute," he said finally. I heard him put the receiver down.

What was I going to do next? I had Mr. Big coming on the line and I had some cards to play, but I didn't know what the stakes were.

There was a rattling on the other end of the line, then another voice came on.

"Lenny told me what you said. Just who the hell are you and what do you want?"

"Who I am is none of your damned business. I'm just a concerned citizen. What I want is safe passage for the girl and her baby and a payment to compensate her for the loss of her husband. Otherwise I turn what I know over to the Feds and you guys are in a world of hurt."

I was making this up as I went along, but liking how it came out.

"What kind of payment?"

"Half a million," I said, picking a number out of thin air.

"You're full of shit."

"Listen, you popped her husband by accident 'cause you can't even tell your good blacks from your bad ones. She and her husband hadn't done shit to you. What do you expect her to do now? Man, you *owe* her." If nothing else, mob people were usually family men. I was hoping they had a weak spot.

"What do I get in exchange?"

"My silence."

"Why the fuck should I trust you?"

"Because if I blow on you, I know you'll track the girl and kid down. As long as they stay safe, I stay quiet. As long as I stay quiet, they stay safe."

I realized as I spoke that if this went down, I was pissing away the story of a lifetime and maybe any chance at working again, but I didn't care. If I could help Latoya and the baby get set up and safe, then that was enough good to come out of this shitty deal. They weren't part of this mess and they deserved to get out of it and away.

"Let me talk to my people," he said.

"I'll call you at this number at noon," I said. "Have the answer I want to hear or I call the cops, the DEA, and the FBI, and they'll be all over your damn bar and dog track."

I hoped that he would take what I said at face value and assume that I knew more than I did. Paranoia has deep roots in the criminal heart; it takes only a little water for it to blossom like a weed.

"Don't threaten me," he said.

"No threat, just facts," I said, paraphrasing from the old Walter Brennan show, and hung up the phone.

I stood there by the pay phone outside the Winn-Dixie, feeling bone-weary, wet and dirty, and scared shitless.

What was I doing? I was going to get myself killed trying to rescue a woman and baby I hadn't even met until two days ago.

I had gone for too many years not really caring if I lived or died, going through friends and relationships like Kleenex in flu season, leaving a trail of wreckage behind me, wallowing in booze, half-heartedly trying to drink myself to death, driving beltless at ninety miles an hour looking for just the right concrete bridge piling to plow into, but too afraid to ever do it, too much in love with myself and my self-loathing to ever do it. I had stumbled onto a cause here. It wasn't my cause and it wasn't a pure cause, but it was something and it was in my lap and I was going to do something about it. Maybe it would help me look myself in the mirror if I lived.

18

Friday Morning

AFTER a shower and shave and some dry clothes, I felt more alive again. Latoya and the baby slept in the back bedroom. Mrs. Copley had some coffee waiting in the old percolator by the time I had dressed. She sat out on the screen porch in my father's wooden rocker. I came out on the porch and sat in one of the other rockers beside her in the gathering dawn.

"Mighty nice out here," she said.

"My father built this cabin," I said. "Or at least he had it built. It was his fish camp in the summers. We went bird hunting in the fall off in the bottom land downstream."

"Mighty nice."

"You should be safe here. Only a few folks know

that this place still exists and you can only see it from the river."

"Why are you doing all this, Mr. Ingram?" she asked, still rocking and staring down at the river running past black as night.

I considered this. "I don't know," I said. "It's the right thing to do. I need to do a few right things if I'm going to be able to stand living with myself."

"You going to sell this story to some magazine or TV program and leave us high and dry?"

I shook my head. "No one would believe me. And that would make me an even bigger target than Latoya."

"I hope you're telling me the truth," she said.

"Yes, ma'am." I put down my coffee. "I've got to go into town and get some things done. I hope to have some better plans as to what to do when I get back."

"We'll be here," she said, then she turned to look up at me. "You got any fishing poles? I'll bet there's some catfish on that river bottom."

I thought for a minute.

"There may be some old poles in the storeroom under the stairs. The key's on the nail by the fridge. Feel free to look around, but watch out for snakes."

She smiled and nodded, then turned back to her rocking.

AFTER two days without any real sleep, I felt like an electrified corpse, animated only by caffeine and adrenaline.

I made the rounds of the sheriff's office and police station. No mention of any shootings out in the county, no bodies, not even a rumor of trouble disturbed the logs from the day and night before. I grabbed another cup of coffee at the McDonald's near the interstate and headed for the hospital, hoping to catch Dr. Hartley in at his usual insomniac hour.

The autopsy room was locked, but I found him upstairs in the pathology offices beside the lab, reading slides at the microscope and dictating reports into a handheld tape recorder. I knocked on his half-open door.

He looked up, at first annoyed, but then he brightened somewhat when he saw me.

"No murders last night, Young Ingram," he said. "What brings you by?"

I fell into the chair opposite his desk.

"Actually there were five murders last night," I said. "But you'll probably never hear about any of them."

Then I told him what I knew of the whole story.

He took the tale in impassively, not betraying even a hint of amazement or belief or disbelief.

Finally he said, "These men are going to kill you. If you let them see you, they'll kill you. That's the easiest way they solve their problem."

"So what do I do?"

"You could do nothing. Forget it ever happened."

He stared at me for a moment, taking the measure of me. He shook his head.

"But you won't do that. You're an Ingram. Maybe you're just finding that out now. You won't be able to put this down. You look just like your father and you're acting just like him. Foolhardy crusading, death wish,

Southern chivalry and bravery." He frowned disgustedly and lit a cigarette.

"You need a better plan than what you've got," he said.

"I don't have a plan."

"Exactly. You need to write down as much as you know and leave it with me. Then you tell these fellows that if you don't come back alive and stay alive, the story gets forwarded to the law."

I nodded.

He pondered, worrying the cigarette between his fingers. "You need to meet these men in an open place with good lines of sight. A place of your choosing. And you need backup. I'm a good shot with a rifle."

"I couldn't get you involved."

"You already did," he said.

"You can't be serious."

"It's the least I can do," he said on. "Your father was a friend of mine. He spent years standing up by himself for lost causes. Always felt bad for not standing up there with him."

I shook my head.

He sighed. "Look, Nelson. I'm an old man. I have prostate cancer. My wife's dead. I've already got my funeral planned and paid for. What the hell do I care if I die tonight instead of next year? You need to do this for some fool reason. You're not the only one. Just let me help you and don't worry about why."

I didn't know what to say to him.

He smiled. "Besides, it might be fun."

"Call me in a couple of hours," he said. "I need to figure out the best way to do this."

• • •

I WENT back to the office and filed a couple of stories and said nothing about what had happened last night. Leyland gave me the evil eye all morning, but left me alone. I drank coffee, and hid in my corner behind the filing cabinets, typing out everything I knew about this story.

Connie came by my desk.

"Did you get them?" she asked, wide-eyed.

I nodded. "They're safe for now."

She bent down. "What are you going to do with them?" she asked in a conspiratorial whisper.

"I'm not sure yet," I said. I had gotten Connie deep enough into the mess and didn't want to involve her any deeper.

"Listen," she said, "I'm sorry for backing out on you last night. It got so deep so fast that I got scared."

"That's okay," I said. "I shouldn't have gotten you involved."

"No, it was great," she said. "I haven't had so much fun in years. You gotta take me along on whatever comes next."

"I don't know," I said.

"Please. C'mon, Nelson, please. I'll do whatever I can to help."

I shrugged. It seemed like volunteers were lining up. "We'll see," I said.

"Great!" she said, smiling. She kissed me on the cheek and bustled off.

At nine o'clock, I called Hartley back at the hospital. He gave me precise details as to the place and time of the meeting, having planned it out in detail.

"Bolligee Road down by the Tenn-Tom," he said.

"Just before dusk. Sunset's at seven-oh-three tonight, so make the meet at six-thirty. Take the license plates off your car so that they can't track you after the fact. Get there early and get your back to the water. That way the sun will be in their eyes. They'll think they have you boxed, but I'll have a ski boat down on the water. Worse comes to worst, you slide down the bank and you'll be out of there quicker than they can follow. I'll be up the draw to the south with a rifle. I can command the whole field of fire from there and I can keep them pinned for quite a while and get out down Gullickson Road before they can figure out where I am."

"Goddamn," I said. "That's good." I was beginning to hope that I might live through this.

"Check back with me this afternoon about two o'clock," he said.

"Okay."

"And when you talk to them at noon, don't tell them where the meet is. Tell them you'll call them with the location thirty minutes before."

"Sure."

He hung up. I held the humming receiver in my hand, feeling as if I had stepped off the edge of a precipice and was in free fall.

A shadow loomed up at the front of my desk. Leyland hovered over me.

"Morning," I said.

He harrumphed. His eyebrows humped up in great piles, his eyes hanging fire at me.

"Copy's been a little thin lately," he rumbled.

I ran my fingers through my hair.

"Yeah, I know. I'm working background on these murders. It's taking a lot of time."

"Those murders aren't going anywhere. Dead is dead."

I stared at him, uncomprehending.

"County commission's meeting tonight. Cover it. And try to get a little substance in the story."

"Sure, Leyland," I said meekly.

"They're having some troubles out at the mall. Two of the stores have closed in the last month. See what you can find out."

"Sure," I said.

He harrumphed again and drifted downstream toward his office.

This was probably going to be my job. I could eke out the mall story this afternoon, but there was no way I was going to make the county commission meeting tonight. I could see another hole blossoming in my résumé, another unaccountable void in my so-called career. Perhaps I would just retire to the cabin and live off the river, fishing for catfish and bass, growing vegetables and making my own corn liquor.

I fiddled at my desk, tried to find something to keep my mind occupied. Time crept by. A little before noon I shrugged into my coat and headed outside, seeking a pay phone to place the call to The Watering Hole.

FROM a pay phone outside the courthouse I dialed the number. The phone rang for half a dozen rings before someone picked it up.

"Yeah," Lenny said.

"Lenny," I said, "this is your friend from this morning."

"Fuck you," Lenny said reflexively.

"Let me talk to your boss."

The receiver clattered down onto a tabletop and a minute passed. Mr. Big came on the line. I told him the terms. He grunted and huffed.

"One car, one person, no guns," I said.

"Sure," he said. "We'll be waiting for your call." And he hung up.

My stomach sank. It was too easy. Something was going to go wrong. I stood at the pay phone, drenched in a sweat far heavier than the midday heat warranted, feeling as if I were in the grip of a lunacy that deepened and became more irrevocable with each step.

I walked back to the office and got on the phone to the business office at the mall, trying to paste together the story Leyland wanted. It was agony. I made a few more calls, scribbled a few notes, then gave up, resolving to come back here to finish the work tonight if I lived.

The phone on my desk rang and I jumped a foot out of my chair. It rang again and I still drew back startled. I managed to pick it up on the third ring.

"Ingram," I said shakily.

"Nelson?" It was Rayburn on the other end.

"Rayburn," I said.

"You okay, son?"

"I'm okay, Rayburn," I said, trying to figure where he was coming from. Did he know something was up? "Why do you ask?"

"You look tired out lately," he said.

"No, I'm okay." It was unlike Rayburn to go directly to such intimacies.

"Nelson, Leyland called me this morning and he's not too happy. Said you've been nosing around, stirring people up. Said you were out at the track and asked a lot of questions and got Riley Hill all exercised."

"I was just working a story."

"This isn't Cleveland, Nelson. Hell, this isn't even Richmond. This is a little town and everybody knows everybody else's business. You've got to tread lightly and show respect to people like Riley."

"Riley's just white trash from Clay Mountain! You know that!"

"Doesn't matter," Rayburn said. "He runs the dog track and he knows lots of folks. He could make things right uncomfortable for you if he wanted. You want to get along, you got to go along."

I gave up arguing. I had no time for this.

"Yes, Rayburn," I said submissively. "I'll try to watch myself next time."

"I've got to play golf with Leyland every Saturday and I'm getting tired of listening to him make digs at you, son. If he didn't lose so much money to me in side bets, I'd give up playing with him at all."

I managed to laugh at this, and promised Rayburn that I would try harder. Placated, he asked if he would see me this afternoon. I begged off, saying I had a couple of stories I had to get done. He was satisfied and let me off. We ended the conversation amicably.

Just before he hung up, I had a sudden sinking feeling.

"Rayburn," I said.

"Yes?"

"Thanks for everything you've done for me," I said.

"Sure," he said, sounding a little confused.

"No, I mean it. Thank you."

"You're welcome."

"I'll talk with you later," I said, feeling my stomach fall as if over a precipice at the emptiness of the promise.

I hung up the phone and got up to leave, ducking out on Connie. This next part was too crazy to involve the innocent.

19

Friday Afternoon

THE air hung heavy and furnace hot, unstirred by even the slightest breeze, the sky a hazy off-white. I was wrapped in sweat before I even got to the car.

I stopped at the hospital and went up to Dr. Hartley's office. He shut the door behind me as I came in, stepping lightly, looking vigilant and excited.

"You make the call?" he asked.

I nodded.

"You didn't tell them the location?"

"No. Not yet."

"Good. Try that on." He motioned toward a cardboard box sitting beside his desk.

I hefted a thick black vest out of the box.

"Kevlar," he said. "Borrowed it from some *acquaintances*. Does it fit?"

"I guess," I said, pulling it on. It was bulky and would be suffocating in the afternoon heat.

"Put it on under your shirt. It'll stop most rounds, but don't think it makes you invulnerable."

"Sure." This was beginning to seem too real.

"Sit down," he said.

He reached into a desk drawer and brought out a silver flask and two shot glasses. Filling the glasses with whiskey, he eyeballed me as I took off the vest and collapsed into the chair opposite him. He tossed back his shot, sucking at the air afterward between clenched teeth.

"You can still back out," he said. "You don't have to do this."

I tossed back the shot, feeling the whiskey burn all the way down, tears stinging my eyes at the biting goodness of it. I pushed the shot glass toward him.

"Another," I said.

He obliged and I tossed that back too.

"I know it's fucking crazy," I said. "But I gotta do it. I've been walking away from things my whole life. For once I'm not gonna walk."

He nodded. "I figured as much."

He pulled out a county map and we bent over it, going over the location, reviewing how I would park, where I would stand, where he would be concealed. I nodded, trying to keep it all straight.

"If they come armed or come in numbers, it's going to be difficult. At the first sign of trouble, I want you to bolt for the bank and slide down to the water. There'll be a boat down there. Crank it up and take off north on the water until you get up to where the Sour Mash joins the waterway. Pull in at the first dock just up the confluence with the Sour Mash. That's my place. The back door will be open."

He looked me up and down, then smiled broadly.

"Goddamn, this is going to be fun." He slapped me on the back. "Now go home and lay down for an hour or two. Try to get some sleep. Call me at five at home and we'll make final plans."

He pushed one of his business cards into my hand with his home number scribbled on the back.

I pulled the notes from my pocket and handed them to him.

"This is all I know about what's happened." Across the top I had written Jack Edmonds's name and number at the FBI. "If anything happens to me, give the notes to him."

I ROLLED down the road to the cabin, honking my horn twice as a warning. Mrs. Copley sat on the riverbank, fishing pole in hand. I parked and walked over to her. A bucket full of catfish glistened wetly beside her.

"Told you they was down there," she said, smiling.

She seemed perfectly at home there along the tree-lined riverbank, the Sour Mash drifting past her silently.

"I could just stay right here, Mr. Ingram," she said.

Latoya came out of the cabin and stood above in the open doorway, holding little Reggie in her arms and eyeing both of us darkly.

I sat on the bank beside Mrs. Copley.

"Been quiet out here?" I asked.

"Quiet as the grave," she said softly. "I hope you don't mind, but I called my sister. Someone came by last night and went through my house pretty good. Broke all the windows out of the front."

"Did you tell her where you were?"

She shook her head. "Don't really know where I am."

Latoya clumped down the steps from the cabin and settled onto the bank beside us.

"So what you gonna do with us, Mr. Reporter?" she asked, unloading the sleeping baby into my unsuspecting arms.

I tensed for a moment at the unfamiliar bundle, but Little Reggie nestled in and turned his head, resting his cheek against my chest. I was smitten. He smiled toothlessly in his sleep, and a burble of curdled milk bubbled up and ran down his cheek and onto my shirt.

"Hold his head up higher," Latoya said. "I just fed him. Hold him like that and he'll be up-chucking all over you."

I hoisted him up higher. He opened his eyes and looked at me, his eyes crossing and uncrossing. He smiled and blapped some more milk down his chin. He flapped his arms around triumphantly, thrashed his legs, and grinned again.

"He likes you," Latoya said.

"I like him, too," I said.

"You got any kids?" she asked.

I shook my head.

"They change your whole damn life," she said, wiping at his chin, smiling ruefully.

I handed the baby back to her. He held out a perfect little brown hand and grinned.

"So I asked you what you gonna do with us?" Latoya said again, staring hard at me.

I looked back at her and explained my plan.

After I had finished, she stared at me wordlessly for a moment.

"You crazy," she said. "You batshit crazy. Those motherfuckers will kill you dead."

"Maybe."

She rolled her eyes. "Yeah, and maybe the sun's gonna set this evening."

"You got any better ideas?"

"Just take me and Little Reggie to the bus station. I'll get a ticket back to L.A. and that'll be the end of it. Once I get back to Compton, those fuckers won't mess with me. They don't have the balls to come down to the 'hood."

"A baby, no husband, no money, and stuck in the 'hood the rest of your life. That sounds like a great plan too."

"Why the hell should I trust you?" she asked, growing heated. "If they don't kill your white ass, what's to keep you from taking all that money for yourself?"

"Nothing," I said. "You'll just have to trust me. What the hell do you have to lose? You can always catch the bus to L.A. later."

"Bullshit," she said. "This is bullshit."

"I don't give a damn about a lot of things," I said. "But I want to give a damn about this. I don't even know why."

Mrs. Copley looked at us both and shook her head.

"I don't know what the world's coming to," she said. "Mostly I wouldn't trust a white man to do anything but look after hisself. But I think we gotta trust you, Mr. Ingram."

"Thank you," I said. "Now, I've got a few hours to kill and I haven't slept in two days. I'm going to go lie down. Make sure I'm up by quarter-to-five."

Mrs. Copley nodded. I turned and walked up to the cabin. It was stifling even with all the windows open. I lay down on top of the sheets on my bed. Weariness seemed to leak from my pores, my body felt as heavy as lead, my muscles ached. I slept fitfully, waking every few minutes to look at the clock.

I awoke to see Latoya's face opposite mine, her brown almond eyes watching me, smoldering. I felt pierced again by those eyes.

For several moments we did not speak, and then she said, "You a crazy son of a bitch, aren't you?"

I nodded. "Yes."

"You rip us off, and I'll kill you," she said evenly, then leaned forward and kissed me.

She rocked back and eyed me again. "You hear me? I'll kill you."

I nodded. "Yes, ma'am," I said, still feeling the heat of her lips. I marveled at her, my killer angel. I had to make sure that she and her boy made it through this and got out of here.

"You get your ass killed and I'll spit on your grave," she said.

"Yes, ma'am." On second thought, maybe I should send her down to meet the bad guys.

Mrs. Copley came into the doorway, holding Little Reggie.

"What you doing, Latoya?" she asked.

Latoya looked back over her shoulder.

"Putting the fear of God into his white ass," she said, then turned back to me and winked.

"What time is it?" I asked.

"Time to get your white ass out of bed," she said, smiling.

I stood and went to the bedroom closet. In the back of the closet behind my clothes, I pulled out the canvas and leather case that held my father's shotgun. I laid it on the bed, unzipped the case, and pulled out the old Mossberg. Rayburn had given it to me right after my mother's funeral.

"Thought you might want it," he had said, half-apologetically.

I had taken it, cleaned and oiled it, and then put it away in the closet, not sure if I really wanted it around. I held it now in my hands.

"That all you got for firepower?" Latoya asked.

I pulled out a box of shells and began to load the gun.

"It'll have to do," I said. Perhaps this gun, which had ended my father's life, could be put to better use this time.

20

Friday Evening

I STOOD at the dead end of Bolligee Road, at the edge of the Tenn-Tom Waterway, sweating under the Kevlar in the full heat of late afternoon. The sun hunkered down toward the west, but seemed to have lost none of its power. A hot breeze stirred through the tall grass; the Tenn-Tom ran past, muddy brown, coursing straight as a ruler south, a single coal barge trafficking slowly to Mobile Bay.

A cloud of dust still hovered in the air along the road and around the car as it sat ticking and creaking. Open fields peopled only with grass and live oak and scrub pine lay all about. To the south a low hump of hills perhaps fifty yards off ran parallel to the road. Somewhere in there, holding the high ground, I prayed, was Dr. Hartley.

Sweat soaked through my clothes. My mouth felt dry and filmy. My stomach gurgled and jumped. I had made the calls, dressed out in the Kevlar, and made my way here.

I checked my watch. Still thirty minutes to go.

Pacing beside the car, I tried to get my bearings.

I had parked the car astride the dead end of the road and now stood with it in front of me, my back to the canal. From the car to the edge of the canal lay about ten feet of open ground. I could turn, cross it in two strides, and be gone down the bank. Standing at the edge of the bank, I craned my neck again to pick out the motorboat lying snug in among the branches.

Minutes passed like agony.

I paced and cast my eyes about, first eastward down the approach of the road, then southward toward Hartley, then westward to stare into the setting sun, then to the blue-white dome of the sky itself, importuning God to watch over this fool's crusade.

Fifteen minutes before the meeting time, I picked out a rising column of dust down the road.

A triad of cars came down the road in a chevron formation—a black Cadillac flanked on either side by full-sized black Oldsmobiles.

As they saw me, they slowed then coasted to a stop right up against my car, sitting with engines running, clouds of dust following behind and now past them, swirling lazily about us all. The windows of the cars were heavily tinted and I could not see inside.

I pulled myself up close to Hubert, my stalwart Ford protecting me from all this General Motors steel, and cast glances over my shoulder, measuring the distance to the bank.

The doors of the Oldsmobiles popped open at once. Three men got out of either car, dressed in black suits, white pressed shirts open at the neck, dark hair slicked back on their foreheads, sunglasses shielding their eyes. They began drifting left and right, toward my flanks.

"That's close enough," I said, my voice high and tight.

One of the suits off to my left smiled wolfishly, and raised an open hand.

"Sure," he said. "No problem." The accent was New York or New Jersey.

"Did you bring the money?" I asked, struggling to pull my voice into a lower register.

"Sure," the wolfish suit said. "Relax."

The right rear door of the Caddie opened.

An older, stouter man climbed out and stood beside the car. The cut of his suit was more expensive. He wore a crisp gray necktie, and as he raised a hand to smooth back his hair, gold cuff links sparkled in the sun. Pushing the door closed behind him, he walked up to Hubert and leaned against the passenger door, regarding me across the roof of the car as I leaned against the driver's side.

He smiled at me, a gold incisor flashing, but said nothing. The suits on either side drifted further toward my flanks.

"Do you have the money?" I asked.

He regarded me silently for long moments. At last he moved to speak.

"Just who the hell are you and why should I be giving you a quarter of a million dollars?" he said evenly in a Jersey accent.

"I believe the figure was half a million," I said, trying to match his cool.

His eyes narrowed.

"Fuck!" he said. "You think I care? I am seriously put out about having to come down to this shit hole since these unfortunate events began to pile upon us. So just tell me why I'm wasting my time here with a cheap shit like you?"

"Because you and your boys fucked up!" I said, warming to my role. "You popped the wrong guy. He hadn't done shit to you. He had a wife and a kid who hadn't done shit to you. You *owe* them. You and your boys have been right sloppy around here for the past few days. Maybe you think nobody's watching or nobody cares. But I've been watching and I care. I know enough about your organization to put you all away, and I'm gonna make sure you pay what you owe to that girl and her kid."

"And who the fuck might you be? What's your angle?"

"I don't have no fucking angle," I said. "I don't care if you guys run drugs from here to eternity. If not you, it'll just be someone else. I don't care. I'm just a concerned citizen who wants you fuckers to do right by this woman and boy this one time.

"I got lymphoma," I went on, getting into a groove, stealing a line from Hartley. "I got six months to live and I don't care if I die this afternoon but I want to see some good come of this whole fucked-up business."

"What the fuck do you know that I should be so afraid of you?"

"Your fucking dog track's a front for drugs. You've been having a turf war with those crazy dudes from LA. A lot of bodies been piling up. I've got names, I've got dates, I've got places."

I stopped there. That was all I had, but I couldn't let him know that.

He squinted at me, trying to make out my face against the glare of the setting sun at my back. His face was haggard but tan, coarse black hair combed back in an outmoded pompadour, gray streaking the temples. He smiled uncertainly, then laughed.

"You're going to have to give me more than that for your half a million! What do you say we go back to my place and we can discuss what you really know?"

He nodded to his men and they began to move around both ends of the car.

My heart gave a big pump and flopped over in my chest.

This wasn't going at all like I'd hoped. I glanced back and forth at the black suits swarming around my car. There was no way Hartley could contain this. No way I could get away in time to scurry safely down the bank. No way I was going to survive this.

I reached down into the open driver's side window of the car, grabbed my father's shotgun, and took a step back, aiming squarely at the belly of Mr. Expensive Suit standing against the passenger side door.

The flanking suits hesitated then drew back behind the protection of Hubert's hood and trunk, simultaneously producing, as if by magic, ugly, short-nosed, machine pistols with a great hubbub of safeties clicking off and magazines shuttling into place. Mr. Expensive Suit took half a step back from Hubert's open window.

"Now why don't we all just hold what we have?" I said loudly. "I don't have shit to lose, like I said before. While Don Vito here probably is fond of his guts right where they are." My hands shook; sweat poured off me like rain.

"Okay," Don Vito said. "Settle down. We can talk here. We can work this out."

I took a step backward toward the bank. "The only way we can work this out is if you've got half a million dollars on you."

He shrugged. "Put yourself in my shoes," he said. "I ask my people back home for five hundred grand to buy off a guy who might not know anything, they're gonna laugh in my face and chalk me up as a first-class dumbski."

"That's your problem," I said. "I got my own issues." I edged another step backward toward the bank.

He smiled. "My problems are your problems," he said and nodded.

A blow struck me in the back of the knees. My legs buckled, the shotgun jerked upward then was struck from my hands.

The gun twisted and spun in the air, the stock falling away from my grip, the barrel turning to face me, spinning as if in a dream.

"Let it happen," I thought as the gun fell and swiveled to face me.

Let it happen just the way it happened the first time, let it end right here.

I fell forward.

The muzzle stared me in the face as the stock struck the ground.

I grimaced, waiting for the flash of smoke and fire.

Let it happen now.

But nothing came.

The gun bounced once on the stock, then fell off to the side. Another blow came hard into my kidneys and I settled to the ground, catching myself on my hands and my knees.

"I want the fucker alive!" a voice shouted.

A foot struck me in the side, driving all the air from my lungs. I toppled on my side.

The next kick came square in the stomach. There was no air left in my lungs, so I grunted noiselessly and rolled onto my back.

A wiry young stud in a black suit stood over me, smiling. Somehow he had flanked me, creeping through the bushes along the bank of the Tenn-Tom to come up behind me.

He pulled a rope from a coat pocket and knelt beside me just as his pressed white shirt exploded in a bloom of red, the dry report of a rifle following close behind. He jerked backward, a dazed and unfocused look on his face.

A second blotch of red erupted higher in his chest, followed by the crack of a second rifle shot.

He crumpled to the ground beside me.

Rifle shots began to pepper the suits by the cars and they scattered for cover, hunkering down beside the cars, ignoring me now and trying to figure out where the fire was coming from. A bullet struck one of the

Caddie's tires, which gave way with an explosive hiss. The suits began to return fire blindly, cursing and ducking.

The pain backed off a bit. I looked around. I coaxed some air into my lungs.

The edge of the bank lay two feet away. The suits crouched around the cars, peering off into the woods. For a moment I was forgotten.

I grabbed the shotgun, pulled it to my chest, and rolled quickly over the edge. A hail of fire followed after me, whizzing in the air over my head as I skittered down the bank. I could see the boat. There seemed to be a pause in the rifle fire from the trees.

"Get that fucker!" I heard from up on the road.

I scrabbled down the bank, slowing myself by grabbing at the branches and bushes.

I stood and ran. The boat beckoned.

I heard cursing from up on the road, then automatic weapons fire peppered through the brush around me. Something bit me through the thigh, then a run of blows hit me across the back.

Hartley's fire from the woods picked up again. The suits cursed and hit the dirt.

I dove for the boat, cleared the gunnel, and rolled onto the deck.

Shots peppered the water around me.

From the deck I reached up and turned the ignition key. The starter motor ground slowly, turning the engine over hesitantly, reluctantly.

"Start. Dear Lord, start," I prayed.

The boat motor groaned and turned. And groaned

and turned. Then caught, coughing and sputtering to life.

I reached up, pushed the throttle forward, and pulled the wheel toward open water. The bowline, tied to a tree branch, pulled back at the bow, then the branch broke and I was free.

The pitch of the engine dropped. The boat lurched ahead, digging into the water, gathering speed.

I pulled the wheel hard, steering out into the channel and downriver, bullets whistling around me. The boat picked up speed and began to hydroplane, pulling up high in the water. I steered downriver, standing behind the wheel, the fire falling away behind me.

In a moment I was away.

I felt deliriously free all at once and laughed aloud. I had failed totally in my mission, but I was alive and away.

I took in lungfuls of air and let loose a rebel yell. Goddamnit, I wasn't dead!

But my leg brought me down to earth. It burned as if it had been run through with a hot poker. I looked down. Blood saturated my pant leg. I felt it pooling in my shoe.

I pulled off my belt and did the best I could to tie it in a tourniquet around my thigh.

The pain spread like brushfire. I pushed the throttle all the way down and hoped that Hartley's house wasn't too far off.

21

Friday Evening

I LIMPED up the bank to Hartley's house nestled among the trees. The bleeding had slowed, but my leg had stiffened, and ached with each step.

The house was a contemporary design, cedar-sided with large windows on all sides. I pulled myself up the steps that led to the back deck, then peered inside.

Nothing stirred.

I tried the sliding glass door. It rolled open on well-oiled bearings.

Cool, dehumidified air wafted into my face. I hobbled into the air-conditioned bliss, pulling the door shut behind me.

A large, open living room and dining room, light and high-ceilinged and airy.

"Hello!" I called out.

The house was silent except for the subliminal hiss of the air conditioning.

The lights seemed to flicker. I felt suddenly cold. A wave of dizziness took me. Leaning against the nearest wall, I settled slowly to the floor. Blackness closed in from all sides. The floor rose up to greet me. The terra cotta tiles felt cool against my cheek.

I AWOKE into a dim half-light. I felt warm.

I lay on a mattress, clean sheets pulled up across my chest. It was dark outside. A murmuring came from the next room.

I tried to sit up, but great throbbing pains in my back and leg pushed me back to the mattress.

"Christ," I whispered, gasping.

I lifted the sheets, half expecting to see no leg at all where the pain lay, just like in the movies. But the leg was neatly dressed, wrapped in gauze, a petite red stain seeping through the outer dressing. I noticed an IV in my left arm, plastic tubing leading up to a bag of fluid hanging suspended from the top of a closet door.

"Hello!" I called out toward the open door to the room.

After a moment, Dr. Hartley stuck his head in.

"Awake, I see."

He walked into the room, pulled up a wooden desk chair, and sat beside the bed. Reaching out to take my pulse, he stared me in the face.

"Didn't quite manage to kill yourself," he said. "Though you gave it a try. If you hadn't been wearing the vest, you might have succeeded. They stitched four rounds into it across your back."

"I fucked up," I said.

"Perhaps. But you're still alive. And only shot up a little. Just a flesh wound in the leg." He smiled broadly. "You were quite a mess when I came in the door—lying in a pool of blood on my good Mexican tile floor. Took some work cleaning you up. Not to mention the floor. I must say that I did okay considering I haven't worked on living tissue for forty years."

"How did you get me in here?"

"Wasn't easy, but William lent a hand and we lifted you up here."

"William?"

He inclined his head toward the open doorway to the room. "Mr. William Charles."

An old black man, dressed in strangely preppy khakis and a blue button-down shirt, stood staring at me. He nodded to me politely, but warily. He stepped forward into the room and offered a hand to me.

"Pleased to meet you," he said, meeting my eyes and not looking away for an instant, sizing me up. "I'm Dr. Hartley's domestic supervisor."

I reached up and shook his hand. "Pleased to meet you, Mr. Charles."

"William is like family," Hartley said. "I'd trust him with my life."

William nodded soberly, but the quick, wary look on his face did not indicate that he currently reciprocated the same level of trust. Bleeding bodies in the living room? Rifles and shotguns lying about? What new depths of madness were these white folks coming to?

William looked from me to Hartley and back again, shifting his weight from one foot to the other uncertainly.

"Yessir," he said at last. "Just like family."

Hartley turned to him. "William, give me a moment with Nelson. We got some things we need to discuss."

William nodded. "Yessir."

He turned and left, looking back at us over his shoulder, still confused. Just like family, he was left out when things got serious.

Hartley got up and closed the door after him, then came back to sit beside me.

"I killed that son of a bitch that jumped you," he said, looking straight at me, his mouth drawn off to one side, puzzled. "I think I winged a second one. Maybe a couple."

I looked back at him. "I'm sorry that I put you in that situation."

"Oh, no," he said, waving his hand dismissively. "Had my eyes wide open. Half expected it. Just glad you didn't get killed in the process."

"Amen to that."

"This is way over your head," he said. "I think it's time to take what you know to the sheriff."

"But we just killed someone."

"Well, we don't have to tell them *everything*."

"What about the girl and the baby?"

"They're alive and safe. That's going to have to be good enough."

"Problem is, I don't know that much. Not enough to convict anyone."

"Enough to get an investigation started. It's not your job to convict anyone."

I shook my head and sighed, wincing at the effort of taking a deep breath. "I know. It's just that. . . ."

"You wanted to prove something, to yourself, to them, to somebody."

"I don't know. . . . It's not right. I just wanted to do something about it."

I tried to sit up in the bed and felt a dizzying rush of pain in my leg and back again.

"The morphine's wearing off," he said. "Here. This will help."

He retrieved an old-fashioned metal and glass syringe from the bedside table, pinched off the IV tubing, and injected a few cc's of something into the IV tubing.

I felt a sudden almost sexual lysis, pain dissolving and a wash of well-being filling me. I settled back on the pillows.

"Oh . . ." I said.

"Morphine's an excellent drug, isn't it?" he said. "It's a wonder the world isn't wall to wall with junkies."

This felt very good. Air flowed in and out of my lungs easily; blood coursed through my body, filling me with a suffused warmth.

"So what do I do?" I asked, all of my cares suddenly distant and arbitrary.

"I'll call the sheriff. He'll send someone out to take a report."

"Okay," I said.

I pushed myself back up into a sitting position. The pain called to me faintly, as if from a distant mountain-top, in a known place but far away. I was wearing nothing but my underwear.

"Where are my clothes?"

Hartley smiled. "I'm afraid they were unsalvageable. I was your size twenty or thirty years ago. I can probably dig out something that fits."

He stood and left the room.

I sat on the edge of the bed, still dazed and lightheaded. Sitting in this couth guest room, breathing cool, conditioned air, wrapped in stiff sheets with their cleanly cotton smell, and in the warm grasp of Morphia, I could believe that the past few days had been a dream. Only the dull throb and blood-tinged dressing on my thigh told me differently.

Hartley came in with an old pair of khaki slacks and a white shirt.

"Try these on," he said as he sat beside me on the bed.

With a single neat move, he pulled the IV from my arm and taped a gauze dressing down over the site.

"We should wait until morning to call the sheriff," he said. "All we'll get this time of night is some pissant deputy."

I nodded. "I need to make some calls," I said.

He inclined his head toward the bedside table, where a phone sat, then left me alone in the room.

I called the river cabin. After five rings, someone picked up the phone, but said nothing.

"It's me," I said. "Nelson."

"Shit," Latoya said, a note of relief in her voice. "You not dead?"

I smiled. "No. Shot through the leg, but not dead."

"Didn't get the money, did you?"

"No, I didn't get the money."

"You okay?" The concern in her voice sounded genuine.

"I'm okay. I'm with a friend. He thinks that I should take this to the police."

She snorted. "I want to be on the bus back to L.A. before you do that."

"What about Mrs. Copley?"

"She's going lay low with some of her people here."

"Okay."

"I'll send someone to get you in the morning. Do you have enough food for tonight?"

"Yeah, sure."

I gave her the phone number here. "If anything happens tonight, you call me here."

Then I called Connie. She answered and her voice brightened when she recognized my voice.

"I've been worried sick about you," she said.

"I'm okay," I said. "Don't worry. I'm at Doc Hartley's place."

"Hartley?"

"Yeah. He's a pathologist, works out at the hospital. An old friend of my family. I talked it over with him and we're going to turn the whole mess over the police."

"Well, that's the first sensible thing I've heard out of you."

"I'll call you tomorrow after I wrap things up."

HARTLEY must have been a rounder man in his earlier years, for the clothes he brought hung loosely on me, the pants staying up only through the intervention of a tightly cinched belt.

Tentatively, I crept out to the living room. Hartley and William sat in twin reclining chairs before the TV set, watching *Matlock*. As I came into the room, William hastily sat up in his chair and stood.

"Please sit here, Mr. Ingram," he said.

I tried to wave him off. "No, that's okay, William."

"No, please," he said, bending over and dusting off the seat cushion ceremonially. "I'll be going to bed soon anyway." He gestured toward the chair, imploring me to sit now. "Please."

Reluctantly then gratefully I settled into the recliner. "Thank you."

"My pleasure," William said, dragging a chair in from the dining room. He sat beside me and attended to the TV show.

Andy Griffith stood in front of the jury in his white ice-cream suit and hemmed and drawled.

"Old Andy got something up his sleeve," William said, chortling.

"Andy's got more up his sleeve than a vaudeville magic act," Hartley replied.

"Watch," William said. "He gonna pull out a rabbit for the jury."

"If Barney could only see him now," Hartley said.

The two of them bantered back and forth like old college chums. Sitting between them, I felt like the odd man out. The show wrapped up with Andy pulling off another courtroom triumph that would have done Perry Mason proud. William and Hartley traded digs and quips. As the credits rolled, William stood and stretched.

"I guess I'll be going to bed now," he said.

"G'night, William," Hartley said.

"Night," William said and headed for his bedroom. "Hope you get some good rest, Mr. Ingram."

"Thank you," I said. "Good night to you too."

"I don't know what I'd do without William," Hartley said sotto voce after William had left. "He was the husband of my wife's housekeeper. My wife died of breast cancer a few years ago. William and his wife moved in to help with her care. After my wife died, William's wife died unexpectedly about a month later. Left the two of us sitting in this big empty house staring at each other. They'd given up their home to move in and help us, so there seemed to be no good reason to change living arrangements."

Hartley sipped at his drink. "I don't know what I would have done without him over these past few years. He kept me fed and warm when I was near crazy after Lacy died."

He coughed and settled back in his chair. "I'm afraid that living with me hasn't been good for him, though. He's read his way through my Harvard Classics. Been dressing himself out of the L. L. Bean and Lands End catalogs. His own see him as uppity and distant. And among whites he'll always be a poor black handyman, no matter how well he dresses. He'll always have to avert his eyes around certain types of white ladies and play the fool around white men. It's gotta tear him up. He's a good man and I owe him a lot."

Hartley shifted in his chair to look at me more directly. "Your father defended Lula Mae, William's wife, back in the fifties. She got some ideas after reading about Rosa Parks. Tried to sit up front in the bus here. Your dad got the misdemeanor charge dismissed. The Klan burned a cross on their lawn and torched their car. That was when your father filed the first civil rights complaint against the Klan. He was hot to teach them a lesson. Lost it in the federal court in Birmingham, lost it again in appeal. Your father didn't have the money to take it any further. Cost him more than money. A lot of folks wouldn't come to him after that."

"I didn't know," I said.

"So, you see, fools' crusades are an Ingram trait."

I sat amazed at the number of lives my father had touched.

"William still talks about what your father did. I felt obliged to help you on his behalf," Hartley said. "At the time, I just sat on my hands and looked the other way. Regretted it ever since. My life's pretty much over, and I thought if I could join in your fool's crusade, maybe the judgment would be less heavy."

He looked at his watch. "Time for your antibiotic," he said, pulling a brown plastic pill vial from his pocket. He shook a bulky white tablet from the vial and placed it on the table beside me.

"I'll get you a glass of water." He rose and went to the kitchen.

"It was a dirty wound," he said, returning with the water. "Best take these for a week or ten days."

He set the vial down on the table. He pulled a second vial from his pocket and placed it beside the first.

"Those are for pain. You can take up to two every four hours."

I downed the antibiotic, then picked up the two vials, inspecting their labels. They were both made out in Hartley's name.

"Thanks for looking out for me," I said.

"Least I could do," he said. "If it hadn't been for me, you probably wouldn't have gone through with this."

He walked back to the kitchen and returned in a moment with two fingers of bourbon rattling around in an ice-filled tumbler.

"I know you're not supposed to mix this with the morphine, but I figured morphine or no, you could use a drink."

"God bless you, Dr. Hartley," I said, "but I think I'll pass." For a change, I just wanted to savor how I felt.

22

Saturday Morning

I AWOKE in the recliner, an early morning light drizzling through the windows. A blanket covered me and a pillow was propped under my leg. For a moment I lay still and awake, feeling safe and at ease. My leg ached, but it was a distant dull pain.

A bustling and clatter came from the kitchen.

Pushing the blanket aside, I sat the recliner forward and tried to stand. My leg protested, roaring now with pain. But it had lost the all-devouring power that it had had last night, and I stood nonetheless. My back was stiff and sore, but in a manageable sort of way. I took a step or two, taking account of myself. Everything moved more or less.

Dr. Hartley came out of the kitchen, followed close behind by an impressive bulk of a man in a khaki sheriff's uniform. It was Sheriff Stanton. He strode heavily, his chunky-heeled cowboy boots echoing on the tile floor.

"Nelson, this is Sheriff Stanton," Hartley said.

"We've met," Stanton said, extending a hand toward me.

His meaty slab of a hand took mine and crushed it in a firm handshake.

"Dr. Hartley tells me that you have some information that might be of interest."

"Maybe."

He perched himself on the arm of the recliner in a casual but studied manner. "I've got time. Why don't you tell me."

I found myself put off for some reason I couldn't identify. His manner of speech was incongruous, his good old boy demeanor seeming forced. He smiled at me broadly, waiting. I sat myself down in Hartley's recliner.

I ran him through the events and what I knew. He listened closely, but took no notes, nodding and pursing his lips. When I had finished, he twisted his mouth off to one side, t'ched, and shook his head.

"Heck'uva story," he said.

"I've got no reason to be making anything up."

"It'll take some checking up on. And a lot more legwork. You willing to testify, if it comes to that?"

I nodded.

"I want you to keep quiet about it for now," he said. "I need to run these names through and make some calls."

He stood and placed his hand on my shoulder. "You did the right thing by coming to me," he said, fixing me with his eyes. "I want you to lay low. You'll be safe here."

He turned and nodded militarily in Dr. Hartley's direction, then walked toward the door. He turned back to us.

"I'll get back to you before today is over," he said, then left.

Hartley and I looked at each other.

"Feel better?" he asked.

"I guess. Probably out of a job, though. I missed my deadline this morning."

"I'll talk to Leyland," he said. "He owes me a couple."

"Thanks, but don't waste too many favors on it."

"I have to go into work," he said. "Will you be okay here?"

I nodded. "What about the girl and the baby?"

"William could fetch them over here."

"That would be good. I still feel like I've got to do right by them."

Hartley turned and called toward the kitchen. "Did you hear that, William?"

"Yessir," William said, poking his head out the doorway.

Hartley took his leave.

William knew of the river cabin and needed only the briefest directions. He nodded and stared at his feet as I described the route. As he turned to leave, he looked up at me.

"Dr. Hartley told me you didn't know how your daddy helped out me and Lula Mae," he said.

"Seems there's a lot about him I didn't know."

William looked me square in the eyes. He was an old man with yellowed sclera. "There ain't many white men I'd miss a minute of sleep over. But your daddy was one.

Couldn't barely stand to be in his own skin most of the time, his own people turned they backs on him, but he spoke up when he saw wrong being done. Wasn't afraid of nothing or nobody."

"I was so young when he died," I said. "I didn't know."

"Well, know it now."

I nodded. He turned and went out the door.

I called ahead and told Latoya to pack up their stuff and be ready to travel when William got there. She was suspicious as usual, but grudgingly complied.

With William gone, I undressed and stood for a long while under hot water in the shower. The water and soap burned and stung in the wound in my leg, but it was worth it to luxuriate under the brisk, cleanly flow, so civilized compared to the limp tepid showers out at the river.

I redressed the wound with some 4x4's and gauze wrap Hartley had left at the bedside, then pulled back on the secondhand clothes, popping a couple of the pain pills to take the edge off things.

In the kitchen I found coffee still warm in the Mr. Coffee. It had gone black and opaque sitting in the pot, and went down like Drano, but somehow it seemed appropriate to the occasion. I limped back to the bedroom and lay back on the bed. The pain in my leg faded as I took my weight off it.

My wallet, keys, and address book lay on the bedside table. I picked up the address book, put the phone in my lap, and looked up Jack Edmonds's number in D.C. If I was going to turn this thing over to the law, I might as well go all the way.

Edmonds picked up his line after the third ring.

"Jack," I said, "it's Nelson Ingram."

"Nelson!" he said, actually sounding glad to hear from me. "I've been trying to reach you. Where the hell have you been?"

"Around. Learned a few things."

"So have I. Listen, that second kid that showed up dead down there, uh, Isaiah Jackson—he was no kid. He was a DEA agent trying to infiltrate an Atlanta gang. The arrest record I pulled was a cover. He and two other gang members showed up down your way to extend their drug distribution turf."

"There seems to be a lot of that going around."

"Yeah. A lot of the gangs have saturated the markets in their home cities. Some of them are looking to spread out."

"Good capitalists."

"Yeah, well, money has its own logic. Anyway, the DEA agent got pulled way out from his backup and got dead before anyone knew what was going on. Local law enforcement was worse than useless in following it up. DEA's pissed and think that the local law's gone bad. Be careful what you tell them, Nelson."

"What?" I asked, suddenly breaking out in a cold sweat.

"The local law may have gone over to the dark side of the force, Nelson. Be careful."

"No shit?" I felt my stomach falling through the floor.

"No shit."

"I just gave up everything I know to the sheriff here."

I could hear the sound of paper shuffling on the other end of the line. "That would be this Stanton fellow?"

"Yeah. Is that bad?"

"He's one of the ones they suspect. Hired to run the county sheriff's office five years ago. Came from New Orleans. Long tradition of bad cops down that way. Seems to be living awfully well on a limited salary."

"Shit. This is bad."

I looked around, half expecting greasy, black-suited wise guys to come busting in from all sides.

"What do I do, Jack?"

"Do you have a place to lay low?"

"Nothing. I'm by myself out here. What do I do, Jack?" My hands were trembling.

"Tell me where you are."

I gave him Hartley's name and phone number, as well as the cabin's phone number.

"Litchfield's an hour or two from Birmingham. That's where our nearest field office is. I'll get on the phone now and get someone out there to bring you in as soon as possible. Lay low until then."

"How long will it take?"

"A few hours at least. Just lay low until we get there."

"Okay," I said, "okay. Just lay low."

"Call me if there's trouble," he said.

"Right. Trouble. Thanks, Jack."

I hung up the phone. I felt panicked and numb at the same time. The coffee suddenly came back on me. I knelt before the toilet and vomited until nothing but dry heaves came, holding on to the porcelain rim, trying to force air into my lungs.

I got on the phone and called the cabin. It rang eight, nine, ten times with no answer.

I tried Hartley's office next, but he wasn't in. I left a

message with his secretary to have him call me as soon as he arrived.

I found the shotgun in the laundry room off the kitchen. William had cleaned and oiled it, but there were no shells to be found. I limped from room to room, looking for Hartley's gun cabinet. In the garage I found a tightly locked metal cabinet with gun oil and rags on the workbench beside it. I rattled the metal doors, testing the lock. If I had had a crow bar, I might have been able to get it open. I scanned the workbench, looking for some tool that would do.

From the other side of the garage door came the sound of tires crunching over gravel. My stomach sank again. I crept to the garage door and peeked out through the slit between the door and the wall.

"Shit," I whispered.

A big black Olds was bumping slowly down Hartley's driveway toward the house.

I backed away and looked around. There was a back door out of the garage. I turned the knob and tried to push it open. It resisted for a second then gave way, creaking and groaning loudly enough to be heard into the next county.

The woods came almost up to the back of the garage. I slipped out the door and into the trees. I ran twenty or thirty yards in, as fast as my bad leg would carry me, then began circling through the woods toward the front of the house. The day was already thunderously hot, and soon I was soaked in sweat. I crept from tree to tree, trying to move quietly, watching the house.

The Olds stood close to the garage. A bulky-looking man in a dark suit sat across a front fender of the car, a stubby-looking machine pistol dangling casually from one hand. The front door was flung wipe open.

I sat behind a legustrum bush. From this vantage, I could peer through the branches and watch the car and the front door and the driveway leading out to the main road. Minutes passed. I became aware of my breath whistling in and out of my nostrils, of the chirping thrum of the cicadas, the sweet heavy scent of the legustrum. Two blue jays crashed from tree to tree, cackling and crying at each other.

The bulky suit with the machine pistol moved from the car fender, navigated an arc around the drive, peering into the woods, then settled down in the shade of the front steps, wiping his brow with a handkerchief.

Amid the distant rumble of traffic on the highway came the sound of a truck slowing, a big throaty engine protesting as the driver downshifted. The pop and crunch of gravel under tires followed. Through the trees at the far end of the driveway I could see Hartley's big gray Suburban rolling toward the house with William at the wheel.

I stood and tried to wave off the car.

The suit stood and walked out into the drive.

This was enough to spook William. He stopped for an instant, then pulled the truck into a turn in the driveway. The suit let loose a burst from his machine pistol into the air. William had the truck half turned in the drive and now put it into reverse, cutting the wheels to complete the turn. The suit trotted to up to the truck, gesticulating with his gun. The truck continued backing until it was half into the trees beside the driveway. Another air burst from the gun did little to stop him.

William put the truck in first and began to roll forward, heading it out of the drive. The suit cursed, stepped back, and sprayed both tires on his side. The tires blew with an explosive hiss and the truck settled lopsided onto the rims.

The suit rapped on the passenger window with his gun.

"Get the fuck out," he bellowed in a Jersey accent.

The doors popped open. William, Latoya, and Mrs. Copley holding a squalling little Reggie climbed out.

"Get in the car," the suit yelled, pointing toward the Olds.

They trooped meekly toward the car. Two other suits came out of the front door of the house. The three of them huddled for a moment.

"Where the fuck is he?" one of them asked William as he stood beside the car.

"Who?" William asked.

"Don't fuckin' play dumb, Uncle Tom," the bulky suit shouted at William, brandishing the machine pistol. "You know who. Where is he?"

William shrugged.

The bulky suit cracked him across the face with the back of his hand. William took the blow without flinching and glared at him.

"Fuck it," the other suit said. "We'll deal with him later."

They pushed William into the car with the others, climbed three abreast into the front, then pulled away, squeezing the big car past the Suburban and out onto the road.

23

Saturday Morning

THE house had been ransacked. I limped inside and called Hartley's office again. This time I caught him in.

"It's Nelson," I said. "You've got to come quick. The sheriff's crooked. He gave us up. After you left, I called a friend at the Bureau. He said the cops were crooked and that I shouldn't tell them anything."

"Slow down, Nelson," Hartley said. "What now?"

"The sheriff's crooked. After you left, some men came. They kicked in the front door and went through the house. I hid out in the woods, but William came back when they were here. They got William and the mother and the grandma and the kid."

"They got William?"

"And the others."

"They got William? Where did they take him?"

"I don't know. They took him away with the others."

"Sons of bitches!" he shouted. "Those goddamn sons of bitches have gone too far! You stay right where you are. I'll be there in fifteen minutes." And he slammed the phone down.

I limped from room to room, peering down out the windows, unable to sit still. I found a loaded 9mm in Hartley's bedside table and stuffed it into my trousers, feeling a little more secure.

Hartley arrived almost exactly fifteen minutes after we had spoken, leaving his car parked on the far side of the beached Suburban. He blew into the house, fuming.

"I don't know why I ever got myself into this," he shouted as he came in the front door. "Goddamnit! Goddamnit to hell!"

He circled the living room, pulling open drawers, obviously looking for something.

"He's like my goddamn older brother. He's the closest thing to family I got left around here."

He found what he was looking for and headed for the kitchen. I limped after him, saying, "I'm sorry, Dr. Hartley, I should have never let you get involved in this."

"Goddamn right you shouldn't have," he said, marching through the kitchen and the mudroom into the garage. "And those spaghetti brains should have kept their hands off my people. . . ."

He stopped in front of the metal cabinet. He fiddled with a large key ring until he found the key he was looking for, then opened the lock.

The gun cabinet held an awesome collection: Kalashnikovs, M16s, two .44 Magnums, a pair of machine pistols, and what looked like a half-dozen hand grenades.

"Where did you get this stuff?" I asked.

He turned and said, his eyes glinting, "I'm a collector."

"Godamighty . . . why didn't you bring this stuff with you yesterday?"

"Brought a Dragunov—a Russian sniper rifle. I think it got the job done."

"God," I said, "I had you figured for a Johnson Democrat."

"I am a Johnson Democrat. I'm also a Jefferson Democrat and I figure a well-armed civil population is the best protection against tyranny. If everyone carried a sidearm, folks would be a helluva lot more polite on the day to day."

He unlimbered two of the Kalashnikovs.

"Helluva field rifle," he said. "Cheap as dirt, never jams."

He handed me both of the rifles, then pulled a green canvas duffel out from a workbench and began dumping ammo clips into it. He tossed a couple of clips to me.

"Lock and load, soldier," he said.

"Just what are you planning to do?" I asked, trying to figure out how the clips went into the rifles.

He pulled one of the .44s off the shelf, then another 9mm from behind that.

"I'm going to get me a few questions answered by our duly deputized civil authorities, then I'm going to get my people out."

He handed me .44 ammo in speed-loaders, and clips for the 9mm.

"This is crazy," I said. "The FBI's on the way, why don't we wait for them?"

He looked at me like I was the crazy one.

"I've been fucked over by my own sheriff, and you want me to trust the Feds? Why do you think Korea and Vietnam were such cluster fucks? It wasn't because Americans don't know how to kill things. You let Uncle Sam in on this and we'll end up with four dead hostages."

He dumped the grenades into the duffel like so many kiwi fruit.

He zipped up the duffel. "Go get the Kevlar," he said, then marched out the side door of the garage toward the driveway.

24

Saturday Morning

"IS Sheriff Stanton in this morning?" Hartley asked politely.

Hartley and I stood in the outer offices of the county sheriff's department. The desk sergeant eyed us balefully.

"Let me call back to see if he's free," he said.

"Oh, he's free all right," Hartley said, and walked past the sergeant to the offices beyond.

"Now, wait—" the sergeant called out, but by then we were past him and getting up to follow us seemed more than he was capable of.

Hartley strode between the desks straight back to Stanton's office. I tried gamely to keep up with him. Stanton was sitting with two other officers as Hartley walked into the room. Conversation stopped as all eyes turned to look at Hartley as he stood in the doorway.

"Gentlemen," he said, speaking to the officers, "if you'll excuse us, we have some business with Sheriff Stanton."

The officers looked from Hartley to Stanton.

Stanton nodded. "Go ahead, boys," he said. "This will only take a few minutes."

They stood and left.

Hartley motioned me into the room and closed the door after us. He stood before Stanton's desk.

"What can I do for you, Seymour?" Stanton asked.

Hartley leaned across the desk, pulled the 9mm from inside his coat, and pressed it firmly against Stanton's neck.

"That's *Dr. Hartley*, you son of a bitch. Now put your hands flat on the desk here right now or I'll blow your goddamn crooked head off."

"All I gotta do is holler and this room will be full of deputies with guns," Stanton said coolly.

"Not in time to save your ass."

Stanton considered this for a moment, then slowly placed his hands palms down on the desk.

Hartley pulled up a chair and sat down, keeping the pistol trained on Stanton.

"Sit down, Nelson," he said. I sat down in the chair beside him.

"What is all this about?" Stanton asked.

"You know what it's about," Hartley said. "Within two hours of you leaving my place, three spaghetti heads showed up, turned the place upside down, and took William and the black family hostage. Now tell me how that happened?"

"I don't know what you're talking about," Stanton said.

"My contacts at the Bureau tell me that you're office has been stonewalling them and the DEA for months and that they think you're on the take," I added.

He looked from Hartley to me, weighing things.

"I'll tell you what," he said at last. "You and little Nelson put away your guns and leave right now, I'll pretend this never happened."

Hartley stood and reached across the desk again, burying the gun deep in his neck, putting his face up close to Stanton's.

"I don't think you understand," he said between clenched teeth. "My son's dead. My wife's dead. I've got a body full of cancer. I don't care if I die tomorrow. You sold Nelson here out to your mob buddies and got my only friend tangled up in it. Now I want to know everything you know and I want to know it right now. If you don't tell me, I'm going to shoot your crooked Cajun head off right here. Do I make myself clear?"

Stanton met Hartley's stare for a long moment. Hartley's nostrils flared, his chest heaved. Stanton looked down.

"Okay," he said quietly.

Hartley sat back in his chair.

Stanton cleared his throat, still looking down at his desk.

"It didn't seem like much at first," he said. "They wanted to be left alone. That's all. Just left alone. In return, they promised me that my county would be free of drugs—no drugs from them or anyone else. It didn't seem like much."

"And the money wasn't too bad either, wasn't it?" Hartley said.

"What were they doing?" I asked.

He shrugged. "I don't know. Didn't want to know. I know they killed those colored boys 'cause they were trying to deal drugs. I didn't have no trouble with that."

"Except one of those boys was a DEA agent from Atlanta," I said.

He nodded. "Nothing I could do about that," he said. "Didn't make him any less dead, and I was getting in too deep." He threw up his hands.

"So where are they?" Hartley asked, still seething.

Stanton considered the question.

"Could be two or three places. They got that club out by the lake."

"I don't think they'll go there," I said. "They know that I know about that place."

"They've got some warehouses down behind the dog track. I don't know what they keep there, but it ain't dogs. They keep pallets of something in there and load them onto southbound barges about once a week."

"Show us," Hartley said.

Stanton reared back in his chair. "Now, look—

"No, you look," Hartley said, leaning forward with the pistol again. "You're going to take us there and show us everything you know. If you do that, and you make me happy, and I get my people back, not only will I let you live, but I will forget everything I know and let you leave the county quietly. If not, and I don't kill your ass, I'll turn you over to the goddamn FBI. And believe me, they've been waiting for something on you."

Stanton pulled his mouth down into a frown, and sat for several long moments.

"What the hell. It'll be a pleasure to help take those bastards down."

Hartley smiled thinly. "That's better." He slipped the pistol into his coat pocket. "Try anything funny in the squad room and I'll shoot you dead."

Stanton shook his head wearily.

"No problem," he said.

Hartley turned to me. "Give us a minute, then you follow. If this bastard tries anything, that squad room will be like a shooting gallery. If you hear gunfire, hit the floor."

I nodded, dry-mouthed, not sure what Hartley would do if Stanton did try anything. I half believed that he really wanted to go down in a blaze of gunfire.

They left, Hartley walking close behind Stanton.

I stood awkwardly in the office, watching the second hand sweep out a minute on the wall clock.

What sort of bad craziness had I gotten myself into—gunfights, kidnapping, blackmail? I was in too deep to back out but scared shitless to go on. A minute passed by the wall clock, then two minutes.

Finally I opened the door and walked out to the car.

25

Saturday Evening

HARTLEY, Stanton, and I stood side by side on a rise of a hill overlooking the dog track, which lay about a thousand yards away nestled into a curve of the Tenn-Tom Waterway. Beyond the track, tucked up against a dense wood, sat the two warehouses Stanton had mentioned.

"You could come in down County Road 28 and cross those woods," Stanton said. "That would put you at the backside maybe fifty or a hundred yards shy of the south building."

Hartley peered through binoculars at the terrain below, then handed them to me. I could see a pair of metal-sided squat warehouses sitting on a large concrete apron, loading bays at one end closed up tight. A broad concrete ramp sloped gently down to the waterway. At the far end of each building was a set of office doors and a row of windows. In front of the second building a long black sedan sat. A figure in a dark suit sat with one haunch perched on the front fender, smoking listlessly.

"Have to wait until dark to get anywhere near the place," Stanton said taciturnly.

"The less you say, the better," Hartley said.

Stanton harrumphed. "Suit yourself."

"Nelson," Hartley asked, "how many guns do you think these bastards have?"

"Seems like I've seen at least six different guys. Who knows, could be more."

Hartley put down the binoculars. "You know how to get in touch with them?"

"I could try the number at The Watering Hole."

"Why don't we call them right in there?" Stanton said, gesturing toward the warehouses. "I can get you the number."

"Just as soon they didn't know that we know where they are," Hartley said. "Don't want them any more twitchy than they have to be."

We lay side by side on the rise, pondering glumly together. The afternoon heat hung about us. Hartley cursed and spat.

"Shee-it, Nelson," he said, "why don't we just knock on the goddamn front door?"

"Yeah, right."

"You know you're going to have to kill them all," Stanton said.

Hartley and I turned to look at him.

"These sons of bitches have long memories," Stanton went on. "You let any of them live and word will get back to their bosses and someday we'll all wake up at the bottom of the lake."

"Then we'll kill them all," Hartley said phlegmatically.

"There's got to be a better way," I said.

"Happy to listen," he said.

"Let me think," I said. "Let me think a minute."

Hartley stood slowly.

"I think we need to deposit the good sheriff somewhere out of the way," he said. "Then we need to sit down and make some plans."

NIGHT had fallen, full of the thrumming of cicadas, the chirp and croak of frogs, the clack and cries of nameless critters. I knelt in the tall grass along the highway, cradling my father's shotgun in the crook of my arm, feeling the night alive all around me.

Hartley had just dropped me off on County Road 28 and sped off. The woods in front of me were a dark shadow. Down the slope, a few hundred yards away, lay the warehouses. Despite the dread possibilities, I felt an unearthly calm. Despite the humid funk of this summer night, I felt as if I were breathing alpine air, moving smooth and easy in and out. Despite the incongruity of finding myself here with assault and murder in mind, I felt a grim determination, no doubt fortified by the three Vicodin I had taken before heading out. I stood and made my way into the trees, my leg aching only enough to make me feel ornery and loaded for bear.

• • •

HARTLEY and I had taken Stanton out to the river cabin and left him out of harm's way, handcuffed to the pipe that ran from the propane storage tank to the house. Hartley figured that was the one thing out there that he might think twice about trying to break free from. Hartley and I had then gone back to his office and made a few calls.

Later in the afternoon, we stopped at a pay phone at a minute mart. I called The Watering Hole and my old friend Lenny answered the phone.

"Yeah?" Lenny said.

"Lenny," I said, "still got wonderful phone manners."

"Who the fuck is this?" he asked.

"You kidnapped the wrong people, Lenny. First you hang the wrong person, then you fuck up my ambush, now you kidnap the wrong hostages. Lenny, where do you get off calling it *organized* crime?"

"It's Mr. Wise-ass," Lenny says, finally putting two and two together.

"I want to arrange a trade. Me for them. Let them go, and I'll give myself up."

He did not answer.

I went on. "I know you don't have the balls to make that call on your own. Why don't you check with your bosses and I'll call you back in ten minutes."

When I called back, he said, "The warehouses behind the dog track. Be there. Seven o'clock."

"Nine o'clock."

"Don't fuck with us."

"Don't fuck with *me*. Nine o'clock or you can keep your four little hostages while I go call the FBI."

"Okay," he said, "nine o'clock. Come alone." And he hung up.

AT the bottom of the slope the woods thinned and the silhouettes of the warehouses loomed from the darkness. I crept to the edge of the trees and hunkered down.

A bulky man in a dark suit sat on the back hood of the black sedan parked on the concrete apron near the office door at the front of the building. I hung back in the shadows of the trees, watching the man in the suit wriggle and sweat in this thick summer heat. The blood pounded in my ears like the beating of a tympany. My lungs pulled on the air as if I stood at the top of Everest.

He stirred, turned his back to me, and stared back out into the dark. He began fishing in his pockets. He was going to light another cigarette. He fumbled and dropped the pack to the ground. Cursing, he bent over.

Now was my chance.

I slipped from the woods, crept along the back wall of the warehouse, and then soft-footed it across the open space between the building and the car.

He had half heard my approach and paused and began to turn. He went for the machine gun he had carried slung under one arm while he dropped to one knee and spun to face me.

I knelt behind the sedan and fixed him in my sights.

"Don't do it," I said. "Don't do if you want to live."

He hesitated and I knew that I had him. He let the gun drop again to his side.

"You're late," he said.

"Lenny?" I said. "That you?"

"Whadaya think, wise-ass?"

"I thought you were minding the store back at the bar."

"I came back here to greet you."

"You're very thoughtful."

"Fuck you."

"Fuck you, too. But enough of the niceties. I want to see the hostages."

He inclined his head toward the warehouse. "They're inside."

"Show me."

"Come inside."

"No. You bring them out here."

Lenny stood slowly. He adjusted his coat lapels, shot a sleeve, tugged at a cuff link, and straightened his tie.

"Let's knock and ask," he said.

"Let's drop the gun first," I said, pointing at the machine gun.

He smiled wolfishly and pulled the machine gun strap off his shoulder, letting the gun drop to the ground.

"Kick it this way," I said.

He raised a foot and kicked it disdainfully in my direction. I bent down, picked it up by the strap, and slung it over my shoulder.

"Now go ask," I said.

He turned and walked toward the door. I fell in behind him, burying the muzzle of the machine pistol between his shoulder blades. He glared at me over his shoulder.

He knocked twice on the door, then three times, and turned the knob, pushing the door half-open.

I leaned the muzzle into his back and pushed Lenny into the open doorway, using his body as a shield.

"Yo! Mr. Wise-ass is here," Lenny said.

A couple more slabs in suits sat with their feet up on a battered metal desk. They glanced up at Lenny, then did a double take when they saw me close behind him looking over his shoulder.

"And Mr. Wise-ass has Lenny's gun," I said, "and he'll drop him if you two so much as look cross-eyed. I'd advise you to sit real still and tell me where my people are."

Both the suits sat stock-still. Finally one of them nodded toward the back.

"They're in the warehouse," he said.

"Bring 'em out," I said.

"What are you gonna trade for 'em? Lenny here?" the bigger slab said, his jaws starting to work a wad of chewing gum again.

"You let them walk, I'll give myself up. That's the deal. I'm the asshole causing you all the grief anyway. I'm the one you want."

"You got that right," he said.

We all stood for several moments, no one speaking.

"So what's it going to be?" I asked at last.

The big slab worked his chewing gum a bit more.

"Do the math, wise-ass," he said. "You kill my dumbfuck brother-in-law, you're bare-assed with nothing to show for it. I got four hostages back there. I can kill two of them and still have plenty to bargain with. Besides that, I don't think you got the stones to pull the trigger." He buzzed on an intercom. "Bring out the girl and the baby," he said to someone on the other end.

The far door to the room swung open. Latoya stood in the doorway holding Little Reggie, another slab in a suit standing behind her holding a pistol on them. Reggie writhed in her arms, screaming and crying.

"Now why don't you just let Lenny go before I lose my temper?" the big slab said.

I wouldn't put anything past them. Latoya looked at me, eyes wide as saucers.

I pushed Lenny into the room. He stumbled and fell to the floor.

"Tell you what," the big slab went on. "I'll let the girl and the kid go. The brat's been crying his head off ever since he got here."

He nodded and pushed Latoya into the room.

"Go on!" he said to her. "Get outta here!"

Latoya moved quickly past me and out the door.

"Go," I told her as she walked by, "straight out into the dark."

She caught my eye. I saw fear and gratitude. I followed her with my eyes.

Lenny was on me before I knew it, up and off the floor and carrying me out through the door and down to the ground.

"Run!" I cried to Latoya.

Lenny drove the butt of the gun into my jaw and a great weight hit me on the side of the head. Everything went white and then black.

26

Saturday Night

MY arms were tied behind me. The side of my head throbbed.

I tasted blood in my mouth. My shirt felt dripping wet and I opened my eyes just as more water splashed me in the face.

I squinted at the lights that shone in my face.

"Mr. Asshole's awake."

"Hey, asshole," said a silhouette looming in my face, shadowed in the backlights.

A meaty hand slapped at me. My cheeks felt swollen and numbed from previous blows.

"You've been a real hair up my ass for the past few days."

I squinted through the glare of the lights, trying to make out his face—shiny black hair slicked back off a low forehead, deep-set eyes, pocked cheeks. He blew cigarette smoke into my face.

This had not gone exactly as I had planned. I had hoped to get all four of the hostages free in exchange for myself. I wondered if Latoya and the baby had gotten away. I squinted and peered around, trying to see if anyone else was with me in the room but could make out only the shadow that still hung over me.

He stepped back and sat on a chair opposite me, knee to knee with me, the bare incandescent light glaring over his shoulder.

He dragged at his cigarette and blew another cloud of smoke at me.

"Now I want you to tell me why you give two goddamns about these pickaninnies, what you know about my business here, and why you think it's worth a half a million dollars."

"Why should I tell you anything?"

He leaned forward and cuffed me with the back of his hand, a quick savage blow that jerked my head to one side.

I tasted blood fresh in my mouth.

"Because I'll have your ass killed if you don't."

"You're going to kill me anyway," I said, trying to pull myself up in my chair.

"Probably. But maybe you can tell me something that'll change my mind. I don't like killing people. It's messy. Makes for ill will. Complicates my business."

"You didn't have any trouble with it this week so far."

I could see his shadowed face pull into a smile.

"After a point I can't ignore things and I have to

make my feelings clear. Our colored friends were warned and warned. Then we strung up one of them and they still didn't see how we felt."

"They were dealing in your territory, trying to muscle in on your turf."

"Muscle in, eh? Is that what you think?"

I shrugged. "I'm not stupid. Not much else worth killing for."

"Is that what you think?" he laughed. "You think we were dicking around over the right to deal crack in Potter County?"

He slapped his knees. "That's good. That's real good."

He got up, walked to the far side of the room, turned back to look at me, and shook his head. "The only thing worth killing anyone over is money. If drugs weren't worth something, you think anyone would give two goddamns about them? You don't know shit."

"I know that you've killed six people in the last week. I know what I saw."

"You also know that five of those bodies are gone and the cops don't even know that they were here in the first place. Besides that, I own the cops."

"The FBI and the DEA have been watching you and federal agents are on the way right now."

"Don't bullshit a bullshitter."

"I called them. They've been looking for an excuse to come in here and roust you and your crooked cops. They're coming."

"Well, then, I guess we can't leave any witnesses, can we?"

He went to a far corner of the room, opened a door, and gestured to someone in the other room.

"Lenny," he said, "get the other two."

After a minute, Lenny brought Mrs. Copley and William into the room. Mrs. Copley's eyes were wide, but William held his eyes tight, sizing up the room. Lenny herded them before him, a snub-nosed machine pistol nestled in the crook of one arm.

I could see my interrogator clearly for the first time. He was the same man who had run things when I met with them down by the Tenn-Tom—a stocky man with a face as pocked and gray as the surface of the moon, eyes lost in the shadows of their deep baggy sockets.

"Untie him," he said, looking past me.

Someone behind me loosened the ropes that bound me to the chair.

"Get up," he said. "I want to show you why you're going to die."

Pain knifed through my thigh as I stood, the Vicodin I had taken now long gone. My head spun, the room rocked and swiveled under my feet, the floor became the wall, then the ceiling, then the floor again as I encountered its concreteness with a dull thud.

"Fuck," he said. "Pick him up."

Hands were upon me, pulling me up roughly. My knees buckled and they pulled me up again before I fell. My legs wobbled and trembled, but held. A pair of bulky suits stood on either side of me, reeking of cologne and tobacco.

"This way," he said.

I was pulled into a warehouse. At the far end sat pallets with large black plastic-wrapped parcels. He walked up to one and sliced open the plastic with a switchblade he produced from a jacket pocket.

"What do you see?" he asked as the suits pulled me close to the pallets.

White gauzy bales lay stacked beneath the plastic.

"Looks like cotton," William said from over my shoulder.

"Very good, Grampa," he said. "Cotton headed downriver to Mobile. Going to mills in Honduras. As legal as church on Sunday."

He reached in between the bales, pushing his arms in past elbow deep. When he pulled his arm back out, he had a plastic-wrapped bundle in his hand. He sliced it open and held it out for me to see.

"Now what do you see?"

Money. Small bills of various ages, tens and twenties.

"Cash," I said.

"Nickels and dimes," he said.

He riffled the bills under his thumb, smiling. He looked at me.

"Crack was a good thing for us. Brought cocaine back to the streets in a big way. Cheap enough for the average stiff to afford, addictive as hell, more profit because we could sell it one hit at a time instead of by the ounce. Smoke it and the rush is twice as good as heroin and ten times as good as a couple of lines of powdered coke."

He stared at the stacks of bills reflectively.

"Problem was," he went on, "that it brought in all these small bills. Fives, ten, twenties—by the truckload. We were drowning in small change."

He turned to look at me. He was enjoying himself. He never got to tell this story and he clearly relished the opportunity.

"You know how most of the big guys go down?" he asked.

I looked at him blankly.

"Money," he went on, not letting the indifference of his audience slow him down. "The Feds track the money. Capone went down on tax fraud. Same for Vasilli, Cartolucci. . . . We had to work hard to launder the cash when we sold cocaine by the kilo. Now we had rooms full of this pocket change. What are we gonna do with it? Make a deposit in the bank? Mail it to my Uncle Carmine in Palermo?"

"So you hide it in bales of cotton?"

He smiled. "It was Tommy that gave me the idea. We went back to Vietnam. He was point man for us in Cambodia and Laos. We used to run heroin out in body bags. He told me about his hometown down South—the real asshole of the universe. And it had this dead empty waterway running straight down to the Gulf.

"So we come down to a county so dull they can't even spell *cocaine,* so clean the DEA just has a white space on their map. We launder a little through the dog track, but most of it we drop in the middle of these bales, load it on barges, float it straight to the gulf, smuggle it out to Honduras, and run it through the hands of some of our friends down there. The Feds are all over Mobile looking for drugs coming into the country. Nobody seems to look too hard for cash going out."

He shrugged.

"You can understand how we got upset when these

black punks tried to start dealing here. We need this area as quiet as Sunday night in Salt Lake City."

He turned and bore down on me.

"And imagine how I felt when you shoved your nose into my business, poking around, fucking up what I worked years to establish."

He pushed me back and I stumbled and fell to the concrete floor.

"I'm laundering cash from all the deals between Detroit and Jersey down this pipeline, and doing a damn good job of it, until you decided you're going to play hero! And now, on top of that, you tell me you called the FBI! Fuck, but you have gotten on my nerves once too often!"

He pulled out a handkerchief and dabbed at his sweaty forehead and neck, shaking his head sadly.

"If you're telling me the truth, then this whole operation is fucked and I got millions of dollars up for grabs on barges between here and Mobile, and years of hard work is down the tubes. If you're shitting me, you have still caused me one giant headache. In either case, you are a dead man."

The two goons pulled me to my feet. It was hard to decide which part of me hurt the worst.

"Take him and the grandma and the old man and cap 'em all," he said. "If you can find the girl and the kid, do them too. They couldn't have gone far on foot."

They hustled us back to the office and out the front door, herding me and William and Mrs. Copley in front of them. We moved toward the big Olds.

Floodlights flashed on from three different directions at once, fixing us like deer in headlights.

We came to a dead stop. Lenny and his partner drew in behind us, looking from side to side.

"What the fuck is this?" Lenny asked.

A figure stood up on the far side of the Olds, silhouetted in the floodlights.

"Let them go," he said.

It was Hartley.

"Oh, Jesus," Mrs. Copley whispered.

"Fuck you!" Lenny said. "I'll kill them here."

He began to pull us back toward the warehouse.

"Let them go, or we'll kill you where you stand," Hartley said and he raised a hand.

A half a dozen pencil-thin red beams streamed in from the dark and settled ruby red dots onto Lenny and his partner's chest and head.

"Fuck," Lenny said. "Laser sights."

He fell back toward the door.

Shots rang out.

A red blossom sprouted in Lenny's forehead.

Blood spattered me in the face. He grunted and dropped to the ground.

His partner spun around, hit in the neck. He staggered but kept his grip on me, pulling me back into the warehouse. William and Mrs. Copley were free as Lenny fell.

"Run!" I yelled and I was pulled back inside, falling through the open door and onto the floor with the gunman on top of me.

He tried to stand and call for help, but he could only rasp. Blood bubbled at his lips.

He pushed himself up to one knee, climbing off me, but then listed to one side and toppled again to the floor.

Shouts and scuffling came from the warehouse beyond the office. I got to my feet.

The Mossberg lay on the desk. I wasn't leaving without it. It was still loaded, the safety off. Hefting it in one hand, I turned to the sound of shots coming from the warehouse. Two gunmen backed into the room from the warehouse, firing.

"Hold it!" I cried, falling to one knee behind the desk.

One of them whirled and sprayed bullets in my direction. They hit the cinderblocks behind me, showering me in concrete dust.

"Nelson!" someone called through the open front door of the office. It was Hartley.

"Stay out, Seymour!" I shouted.

He came in the doorway as another salvo of machine pistol fire stitched across the wall and into the open doorway. He fell to one side, firing his AK47 high and wide.

"No!" I shouted and stood.

I brought the Mossberg to bear on the two men in the far doorway. First one, then another, turned to me. They brought their guns around toward me.

I fired.

Flame and smoke erupted from the muzzle, the shell jacking out.

I fired twice more.

They were only ten feet away and the shots hit them all midsection. They went down in a spray of blood, their shots clattering into the metal desk in from of me and powdering the concrete floor at my feet.

The cartridges were still in my pockets. I reloaded,

then kicked the machine guns away from the two I had shot. They were dead or dying, lying in pools of blood. I didn't look too closely.

More shots came from the warehouse—short controlled bursts of automatic weapon fire. Screams and shouts filled the air.

Hartley lay in the doorway, slumped over. I knelt at his side. He didn't move.

I reached out a hand and rolled him onto his back.

"Seymour?"

His chest heaved suddenly. His lids flickered. He opened his eyes then shut them again.

"Damn," he said. "I'm not dead."

A figure in fatigues and a black ski mask came in from the warehouse, an M16 on his hip. Seeing Hartley down, he quickly crossed the room and knelt at his side.

"It's all clear," he said, pulling off his mask. It was Junior Cunningham.

"This wasn't supposed to turn into a massacre," I said, struggling to stand.

Hartley had recruited Junior and his vigilante militia to back us up. All it had taken to get them onboard was to mention that the targets were a bunch of drug-dealing Yankee mobsters. The plan had been for me to try to trade myself for the four hostages to simplify the math of any rescue attempt, then for them to intercept us as they tried to leave with me. Worse came to worst, they were to rush the building, which it seemed they had just done.

"Collateral damage," Junior said sarcastically. "Looks like you did your share in here."

Hartley pulled himself into a sitting position, grimacing.

"You know we couldn't let them live, Nelson."

There was blood everywhere. Bodies everywhere. Hartley was right. The madness comes from within, in our very genes. What had been involved here to warrant so many deaths?

"God," I said, "how did things get this far?"

Junior hauled Hartley to his feet.

"Just another Ingram crusade," Hartley said. "Although, I must say, yours are a bit more colorful than your father's."

I looked around at the bodies. Just another Ingram crusade.

Hartley looked me up and down.

"Sometimes it's hard to see where you cross the line," he said. "One minute you're offering a fatted calf up to Jehovah, the next you're cutting out the beating heart of your enemy to appease the sun gods."

Junior shook his head. "You're something else, Seymour."

Another man in fatigues came in. "The Feds just rolled into Litchfield. They're at the police station."

"We better scatter," Junior said. "Won't be long before they get wind of this."

"Much obliged for your help." Hartley nodded to Junior.

"My pleasure, Dr. H," he said.

I shook his hand sheepishly.

"I thought you looked like Lawyer Nelson's boy," Junior said to me. "Now don't get the wrong idea. Still don't have much use for coloreds. It's just that the only thing worse than integration is Yankee carpetbaggers."

He pulled out a cigar, lit up, nodded at us both, and walked outside. "Mount up! Move out!" he called and shadowy figures started gathering.

I shook my head. "I never thought I'd be relying on damn right-wing militia."

Hartley harrumphed. "Necessity makes for strange bedfellows. You think Stalin liked cozying up to Churchill?"

"Go get your car and pull it around to the warehouse," I said to Hartley. "There's one more thing I have to do."

I turned and limped back into the warehouse, every ache, pain, bruise, and wound beginning to glow and burn as the adrenaline faded. There were more bodies there, all of them mobsters. Mr. Big lay in the open door of a small office space partitioned off. I knelt over him. He had been hit in the chest and blood soaked his shirt. His eyes were open, staring emptily.

In the office there was a desk and a computer. A box of floppy disks sat beside the computer, an open ledger book in the middle on the desk. I grabbed them and went out into the warehouse again.

I pulled some empty cardboard boxes off a shelf and dragged them over to the cotton bales. I reached into the bale that had been cut open and began bringing out the packets of cash and dumping them into the boxes. Stacks and stacks of bills, endless piles of cash came out of the bale. When that bale ran dry, I moved on to the next. I filled five boxes. Hartley came in as I was trying to close the boxes.

"Holy shit," he said.

"They were smuggling," I said. "But cash out of the country, not drugs in. Drug money out to Honduras to be laundered."

"And what are you going to do with it?"

"I'm going to see that some good comes out of this fucked-up mess." I stacked the boxes and levered them up on an appliance dolly. "Which way is your car?"

27

Monday Morning

HARTLEY and I decided to leave the Copleys out of the whole story at this point. They agreed to lie low for another night at the cabin while Hartley and I would answer all the questions the police would have. We agreed on a minimal story to tell them—I had fallen into the hands of the mob as a result of my reportage. While in their clutches some sort of shoot-out had occurred, leaving my captors dead. I escaped, called Hartley for help. He picked me up on the highway outside of the dog track. I knew nothing other than this. Hartley and William knew nothing at all. It seemed easy enough to remember.

We drove down back roads, taking a circuitous route away from the track to avoid any law enforcement headed our way. For many miles we drove silently.

"What are we going to do with Stanton?" I asked.

Hartley drove for a while. He sighed at last. "Let him go and tell him to make himself scarce."

"You think we can trust him?"

"Hell, no. But if he goes to the Feds, they'll throw him in jail, and if he goes to the other side, they'll probably just flat out kill him. I think we can at least trust him to go to ground and stay there."

We drove down the narrow road to the cabin, pulling up beside it. Hartley trained the headlights on the storage shed. He tossed me the key to the handcuffs.

"You cut him loose," he said. "I don't have the stomach to even look at him."

I climbed out, aching with every step, still hefting my shotgun in the crook of my arm. It was beginning to feel at home there. The Copleys piled out of the back and headed up the stairs to the cabin.

I opened the shed door. In the raking light from the car I could see Stanton still standing where we had left him, arms draped around the propane tank.

"Not dead, I see," he said.

I unlocked the handcuffs. "Can't say that about everyone tonight," I said.

He rubbed his wrists. "What now?" he asked, sizing me up.

"If I were you, I'd hit the road before either side catches up with you," I said.

"I was just caught in the middle, you know."

"You turned your back. You sold us out."

"I didn't sell you out," he said.

"You were the one who told them I was at Hartley's. You were the one who set this whole mess in motion."

He shook his head. "I didn't tell anyone. I was scared shitless after talking to you. I didn't know what I was going to do, but I didn't tell anyone where you were."

"Bullshit."

"Sorry, but it's true. Why would I bother to lie to you now?"

I stood for a moment. "Then who?"

"Don't know. But it wasn't me." He picked his hat up off the floor and walked past me out the door.

Stanton stood in the open air. Hartley leaned out the window and called to him. "Deland is about ten miles up the highway. There's a bus station there. If I were you, I'd be on a bus to somewhere before people start wondering where you are."

Stanton pursed his lips disgustedly and moved off into the dark.

"He says he wasn't the one who sold us out to the mob," I said to Hartley.

Hartley snorted. "Sure. And you believed him. Don't start going soft on me now, Nelson."

I shrugged. We stashed the weapons and money in the rafters of the shed beneath the house, then set out in the car. Mrs. Copley, Latoya, and the baby hunkered down in the cabin with most of the lights out.

WHEN we got to Hartley's house, a group of nondescript government Fords and Litchfield PD cars were parked in the drive, the red and blue lights on the police cars illuminating the scene. As we rolled down the driveway, around the beached hulk of the Suburban, Feds in suits and cops in uniform spilled out of Hartley's house and into the driveway. They clustered around the car, shining their maglites into windows.

Sonny Trottman's face leaned down and he rapped his knuckles on to the window. Hartley rolled down the window.

"Evening, Dr. Hartley, Nelson," he said, smiling broadly and nodding toward both of us. "Understand y'all had a little trouble out here today. Would y'all mind stepping out of the vehicle for us?"

Hartley turned to look at me. "Reckon we should do what they want?"

I nodded. "I've had enough excitement for one night."

I popped open the car door and turned to step out. Every muscle and joint in my body had stiffened. My leg burned as I tried to stand. I pushed to my feet and stepped away from the car. Blood roared in my ears and I felt myself drifting. The dim light of the driveway darkened. Hands reached out from far away and grabbed me but I felt like I was falling.

I CAME to lying again in the bedroom of Hartley's house. Daylight seeped into the room through drawn curtains. Connie sat beside the bed, fretting with something on my leg. She saw that I was awake.

"I was wondering when you were gonna make up your mind and either die or wake up," she said.

Every cell and fiber in my body ached. "I think I died," I said.

"Then you're in big trouble, 'cause I can guarantee you this ain't heaven."

I sat up. Yes. Every cell and fiber throbbed.

Hartley came into the room. "Among the living again?" he asked.

"Barely," I said.

"Police will want to see you this morning," he said. "They found the bodies at the dog track. They would have held us in custody if I hadn't been able to prevail on our friend Chief Bailey to let you sleep it off here."

Rayburn followed Hartley into the room. He stood just inside the doorway, eyeing me with his head cocked to one side.

"Goddamnit, but you are your father's son," he said. "Worse than him. He never got his ass shot off rescuing a pack of dope dealers."

"They weren't dope dealers, Rayburn. They were just people caught in the middle."

"Leyland has fired you twice in the last day and a half," Connie said.

"Given the story you've got to tell, I'll bet he'd be willing to take you back," Rayburn said.

I shook my head. "I don't think I can write this story without putting me and a lot of other people at risk. And I don't know if I want my job back anyway."

Rayburn looked disgustedly over to Hartley.

"I don't know what to do with him, Rayburn," Hartley said.

"What the hell are you going to do?" Rayburn asked.

I stood woozily, reaching out for the wall. Connie was at my side.

"I'm going to take a shower," I said. "Then I'll go talk to the police about all this."

After a shower and a couple of Vicodin I dressed in

another set of hand-me-down clothes from Hartley. Connie came into the room as I finished dressing.

We stood awkwardly for a moment.

"It was you, wasn't it?" I asked.

"It was me what?"

"You were the one who told them I was hiding out at Hartley's yesterday."

"I don't know what you're talking about," she said, taking a step away from me.

I grabbed her by the wrist. "There were only four people who knew I was at Hartley's yesterday. Hartley, William, Stanton and you."

"The sheriff did it," she said. "He was on the take."

"He was on the take, but he didn't sell us out. It was you."

She tried to take another step away. "Nelson, let go. You're scaring me."

"I want to know who you told and why."

"Nelson!" She pulled her hand free and stumbled against the wall. I backed her into a corner.

"I want to know who you told about this and why."

She looked desperately around. "I didn't tell anyone."

Blood roared in my temples. My nostrils flared. I bore down upon her. "I want to know who and why," I said evenly.

She wrung her hands. "I only told Leyland."

"Leyland?"

She started crying. "Ever since you started pushing that story about the lynching, he had me keeping tabs on you. He told me to keep an eye on things and to let him know what you were up to."

I stared at her, still trying to get my mind around things.

"We were just trying to keep you out of trouble. Leyland said there were some stories that just shouldn't be told."

I backed away, my heart still pounding. "And who did he tell?"

"I don't know. I really don't know. I didn't know he was going to tell anybody. He just told me I was helping you and protecting the paper and that I might get a promotion out of it."

She dabbed at her eyes, her mascara beginning to run.

"Go," I said at last. "Get out of here."

"I'm sorry, Nelson," she said. She turned and left hurriedly.

28

Monday Afternoon

BEFORE going to the police station, I swung by the river cabin and checked on the money, still stashed in the tool shed that leaned-to under the house, hiding high in the crooked rafters. I emptied three boxes' worth into a large canvas duffel bag, rough-counting it as I went.

William had already come by and taken the Copleys back to Banfield. Mrs. Copley had left the upstairs cleaner than it had been in years.

In town, I spent a few hours talking with the police and the FBI. I told them as much of the truth as they needed to hear but left the final shootout vague and unclear, and mentioned nothing of Connie and Leyland. They seemed satisfied enough with what they had.

On my way out I ran into Jack Edmonds coming in

the front door of the police station. He smiled at me broadly and reached to shake my hand.

"Nelson, you son of a bitch," he said. "You look like shit."

My hand, bruised from I don't know what, screamed in pain in his grip. "Looks worse than it is," I said. "What brings you here?"

"I got you to blame for that. Because of you, the Bureau thinks I broke this case. They sent me down to head the follow-up investigation."

"That must be a feather in your cap."

"I guess," he said. He looked around the station house glumly. Desk Sergeant Beatty eyed him suspiciously. Well-dressed, cosmopolitan black men were not a common thing around here.

He added, sotto voce, "Working in Richmond was bad enough. I'm not sure I can take this. Man. *Alabama.*"

"It's a long, strange trip," I said.

He told me that they had stopped barges all the way down the Tenn-Tom and had turned up mountains of cash from every cotton bale between here and Mobile. Riley Hill had been taken into custody this morning and all of the files at the dog track had been seized. At the other end, they were trying to follow the trail up through Burmington Southern and its manifold holding companies. Jack made no mention of the curiously emptied cotton bales in the warehouse.

"We need to talk later," he said.

"I don't suppose you want to reminisce about the good old days," I said.

"We can do that too." He smiled and began to walk behind the booking desk.

"Can I help you?" Sergeant Beatty asked defensively.

Jack whipped out his ID without breaking stride. "FBI," he said. "Where's the chief?"

Beatty pointed dumbly toward the back and Jack continued on his way.

From the police station I made my way back to the offices of the *Ledger*. Things were quiet, but the lights were on in Leyland's office and he sat over his desk, peering into his computer.

Without knocking, I walked into his office and sat opposite him at his desk. He looked up, doing a little double take as he recognized me.

"Nelson," he said. "How're you doin', son?"

"Fine," I said evenly. "How about you?"

"Just fine," he said hesitantly. He looked down. "You know, you still have a job here if you want it."

"That's mighty white of you, Leyland," I said. "I'll think on it."

He looked taken aback.

"There's something I need to know," I said, leaning forward. "Just what were you thinking when you sent Connie Perkins to bird-dog me?"

He pushed some papers around on his desk, glancing up at me then looking down again. "You were playing with fire, son," he said at last.

"And just who did you give me up to when Connie told you I was laying low at Doc Hartley's house yesterday?"

He harrumphed and cleared his throat. "Riley Hill

called up. He wanted to know how he could get in touch with you."

"And you told him everything, didn't you? Riley was one of them," I said. "If you'd only listened to me, you'd have known that."

He heaved another sigh. "Nelson," he said, gathering himself, "I didn't need to listen to you. Folks can know things without really knowing it. Sometimes it's best not to know it. Lots of folks around here knew things without knowing it. Don't you think we noticed all those black Caddies rolling in and out of the county? Don't you think we knew what kind of people Tommy Sheehy and Riley Hill were?"

"Then why'd you sell me out to them?"

He was growing angry and defensive. "Money talks, son, and those people brought a lot of it to this little old county. I was trying to look after you, but you kept putting yourself in the line of fire. Past a point, I couldn't protect you."

"You gave me up, Leyland. You turned me over to them. You must have known they were going to kill me."

He looked down. "You were the one who put yourself in harm's way. You were the one threatening to undo whatever good had come from those people coming here. Did you expect me to stand in between you and them?"

I looked at him amazed. "Who else knew about this?"

"Everyone knew. No one knew. Like I said, folks didn't want to know."

The hairs on the back of my neck stood on end. Then

I couldn't trust anyone not to turn me in if the mob came poking around Litchfield to find out what happened.

"Leyland," I said, "what kind of town is this?"

"Just like any other little town down on its luck and ready to take any hand-up that comes by."

I shook my head, then stood.

"You're just like your goddamn father," Leyland said. "You think your shit don't stink, son?"

I leaned over, grabbed him by the collar, and hauled him to his feet. His eyes grew wide.

"If I ever hear you talk about my father again, I'll kick your fat ass all over this town. Do you hear me?"

He nodded, his mouth working like a guppy.

I DROVE out to the Copley house in Banfield. The afternoon had warmed to the forge and anvil heat more typical of a mid-July. Cicadas trilled in the trees.

I walked up the front steps of the house to find Mrs. Copley cleaning the tumbled mess of her front room. The front door had been kicked in and the furniture turned topsy-turvy, drawers pulled out, sofa cushions strewn about, crockery shattered. The chaos had been sitting undisturbed since I had spirited them all away in the dead of night with the mob at their heels.

She knelt in the front room, picking through the wreckage, sifting out the broken pieces and pitching them into the trash. As I came into the room, she looked up at me and pursed her lips ruefully.

"I'm sorry," I said.

She shook her head slowly. "Wasn't your doin'."

"Do you think it's safe to stay here?"

"Lord, I don't know," she said.

She righted her coffee table and set a slightly bent lamp upon it.

"If those people got nothing better to do than to come all the way down to Banfield, Alabama, to kill an old black widow-woman, then I suppose I'll let 'em."

Latoya came out of the back part of the house, carrying a broom. She gave me a hooded, going-away look.

"Hey, Mr. Reporter," she said softly.

"You and Reggie okay?" I asked.

She nodded. "Yeah. We're just fine."

"What are you going to do?" I asked.

"I want to go back to L.A.," she said. "They won't come messing in Crip territory. They'll get their greasy white asses shot off."

"I sure am gonna miss Little Reggie," Mrs. Copley said. The tone of her voice suggested the issue was way past settled and that Latoya's mind was made up.

"How you gonna get there?" I asked.

She shrugged. "Just like I got here. On the damn Greyhound."

"Why don't you just buy a car and drive home?"

"Yeah. Sure. With what?"

I smiled. "Come with me."

We walked out to Hartley's Lincoln. I opened the trunk, pulled the canvas duffel toward us, and unzipped it.

"This is for you and Reggie," I said.

She peered into the open mouth of the bag and her

eyes widened at the sight of the tumbled stacks of five and tens and twenties and fifties.

"Where'd you get this?" she asked.

"From the men who killed Reggie."

She stared at me.

"I figured it was only your due," I went on. "I think it's about two hundred and fifty thousand dollars."

"Shit. . . ." she whispered.

"I did keep a little for myself," I said. "And I'd like to give some to Mrs. Copley to fix up her house."

"What am I gonna do with all this? Any bank's gonna take one look at a nigger with a bag full of cash and know that it's drug money."

"There are ways. Put a little in the bank here, a little in a mutual fund there, open a safe-deposit box at a third place and put the rest in there. You'll transfer the rest into the accounts a little at a time. You invest this well, and it'll work for you for a long time."

She turned back to look into the bag, her mouth still agape.

"This will give you time to figure out what you want to do. You're a smart woman. You should think about going to school, of doing something with yourself."

"Just what's up with you?" she said, mock angry. "Why you keep on showing up here? You don't owe us nothing."

I found myself blushing.

"I'm doing this for myself as much as anything else. I need to see that this turns out as right as I can make it. I just need to. For myself."

I looked down at my feet.

"Please. Take my word. I'm almost forty years old

and I haven't stood up for anything in my life. I stood up for this. I'm not even sure why, but I need to finish it. I've been a screw-up my whole life and I just want to make this one thing right."

"White folks *are* crazy," she said, smiling slightly. She hugged me. I grabbed her and kissed her forehead.

"Take care of yourself and Reggie," I said. I let go of her and turned, blinking away tears.

EPILOGUE

End of June

RAYBURN had towed Hubert in from the riverfront, replaced the tires and the windshield, patched the holes in the exhaust and radiator and oil pan, and gave it back to me in running condition. The bullet holes had been patched with bondo and primer. They looked like gray fishy welts in the battered body of the old car.

I picked it up in front of Rayburn's house after visiting with Aunt Lucille. The engine turned over reluctantly. I drove the old car through the streets of Litchfield and out the country roads to the river cabin.

The heat was intense past all metaphor or simile. I sat on the screened porch in the still of the late afternoon, sweating contemplatively, sipping on an iced tea and watching a thunderstorm boil away to the west. Before me on the porch sat one of the boxes of cash I had taken from the warehouse. It contained about fifty thousand. Enough to tide me over quite a while in my present modest arrangements. Other than food, electricity, and gas, my overhead was practically nil. The ledger and floppies were in there, too. I didn't know what to do with them, but thought that they might come in handy someday.

I rocked in the weathered porch rocker and pondered fate and life and what to do with myself, still a jobless ne'er-do-well now nigh unto forty years old.

The sound of tires rolling down the access road came to my ears. I stood, kicked the box into a closet, picked up the Mossberg, and went to the front door to see who approached, half-hoping it was my Mafia acquaintances come to settle the score and relieve me of my career choices.

It was, instead, Rayburn and Hartley riding up in Hartley's Lincoln.

They rolled to a stop near the foot of the stairs and both climbed out, standing for a moment in the hot green damp primeval summer, drinking in the memories of times past. Finally they noticed me on the upper landing to the cabin, waved, and trudged on up the stairs.

Hartley shook my hand, eyeballing me up and down.

"How's the leg?" he asked.

"Still sore. Stiffens up if I sit too long. But it's getting better."

He grunted noncommittally and moved into the cabin.

Rayburn came up the stairs after him. "Got the car fixed up for you."

"Appreciate it," I said, shaking his hand. "Can I fix you two a drink?"

"A bit early for me," Rayburn said.

"What the hell," Hartley said. "I'm retiring in a month. Fix me a stiff one."

"C'mon, Uncle," I said.

He nodded and I poured them what was left of my George Dickel. We sat together on the porch, taking in the afternoon. It seemed like an hour passed, the river running by, the cicadas singing in the grass, and none of us talking.

Finally, Hartley drained his glass and rocked back and forth emphatically.

"Well, damnit, Nelson, what are you going to do?"

Stealing a trick from Rayburn, I let the question hang in the air, unanswered.

"Don't know," I said at last. "And I'm in no hurry to figure it out."

"I told Leyland some of what happened," Rayburn said. "He's willing to take you back at the paper."

"Don't know about that," I said. I thought it would be winter in hell before that happened.

"Suit yourself," Rayburn said.

Hartley huffed and stood. "This goddamn prostate cancer's eating my bones up. I gotta get home."

"That cancer's been eating you up for ten years and you still look pretty fit to me," Rayburn scoffed. "Just when are you going to get around to dying from it?"

"You want to see the pathology reports?" Hartley asked defensively.

"I'll take your word for it," Rayburn said, rising to leave with him. "But you are the best-looking dying man I ever did see." He moved toward the door. "You coming for Sunday dinner?" he asked on his way out.

"Sure, Rayburn," I said. "What time?"

"Three o'clock. Like always."

I nodded and Rayburn headed down the steps. Hartley lingered at the door.

"You really okay?" he asked, eyeing me like a piece of bad meat.

I nodded. "You know, they're gonna be back," I said.

He considered this. "Maybe," he said. "Let 'em come."

"Leyland was the one who gave us up," I said. "He knew. He gave me up to Riley Hill, and he knew what it would come to."

Hartley looked down. "A lot of people knew, they just didn't want to admit it."

"Did you know?"

"You know how it is with folks. They don't want to know. Down deep we're all just Good Germans. How do you think we got by with slavery for two hundred years?"

"I guess I expect more of people."

He smiled. "Of course you do. You're an Ingram."

Rayburn honked the horn of the Lincoln.

"Let's get going, Doc," he called from below. "I've had enough of this heat."

Hartley reached out and squeezed my shoulder. "Let me know how things go for you," he said and headed for the door.

They took their leave and squabbled amiably as they climbed into the car.

I sat and rocked into evening, listening to the rattling

and chirrup from the woods, the dark gathering slowly. Perhaps I would just keep my watch here at the side of the river, sip a whiskey now and then, keep the Mossberg by my side, and see what developed. At least as long as the money held out. On the other hand, I had this notion that I might go to law school.

Time would tell.